Praise for

"Marianne Martin is a wonderful story teller and a graceful writer with a light, witty touch with language and a sensitivity to the emotions of people in love. There is a tenderness and brightness to her characterizations that make the personalities quite beguiling." Ann Bannon

"*Under the Witness Tree* is a multi-dimensional love story woven with rich themes of family and the search for roots. This is a novel of discovery that reaches into the deeply personal and well beyond—into our community and its emerging history. Marianne Martin achieves new heights with this lovingly researched and intelligent novel." Katherine V. Forrest

"[*Under the Witness Tree*] was entertaining, and the way the pieces all came together was ultimately quite satisfying. Read it for the tight plot, for the mystery, for the romance, and don't miss this engaging story." *Midwest Book Review*

"Marianne Martin is a skilled writer who fully develops her characters and pulls the best from them. . . . *Under the Witness Tree* is a novel rich in character and storyline."
Mega Scene Book Review

"*Mirrors* is a very fine novel, well worth your time and treasure."
The Bay Area Reporter

"Not only does [*Love in the Balance*] have love and excitement, but it has issues very close to all of us."
The Alabama Forum Gaiety

"[*Legacy of Love*] is undoubtedly one of the finest . . . worth reading." *Our Own Community Press*

"[*Dawn of the Dance*] is a beautifully written love story, filled with gentleness and drama." *Mega Scene Book Review*

Also by Marianne K. Martin

Under the Witness Tree
Mirrors
Never Ending
Dawn of the Dance
Love in the Balance
Legacy of Love

DANCE IN THE KEY OF LOVE

BY
MARIANNE K. MARTIN

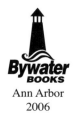

Bywater
BOOKS

Ann Arbor
2006

Bywater Books, Inc.
PO Box 3671
Ann Arbor MI 48106-3671

Printed in the United States of America on acid-free paper.

First Bywater Books Edition: June 2006

Cover designer: Mari SanGiovanni

ISBN 1-932859-17-9

This novel is a work of fiction. All persons, places, and events were created by the imagination of the author.

For Jo

ACKNOWLEDGMENTS

The author would like to offer her gratitude and thanks to the following for their invaluable help in the production of this book:

Publisher and editor, Kelly Smith, whose attention to detail and her wonderful ability to analyze plot and character continue to make me a better writer.

Editor, Mandy Woods, whose keen eye and expertise is so important to the finished quality of this book.

Life-long friend and confidante, Jean Buchanan, whose time and careful analysis was very important to the authenticity of certain character development.

My sister Trish, and Eric, who ping-ponged ideas and scenarios with me until some of them started to make sense.

Graphic artist, Mari SanGiovanni, whose cover art beautifully captures the essence of *Dance in the Key of Love*.

And my best friend and partner, Jo, whose encouragement and support is immeasurable.

Chapter 1

Who is going to recognize me? It's been sixteen years, people change, neighbors move. Paige scanned both sides of the rural road before stopping the car in front of an overgrown cornfield. The only house in sight was tucked behind a large maple tree and rangy forsythia bushes.

She jumped from the car, unlocked the trunk and flipped an old rag over the edge so that it partially covered the license plate, then quickly shut it and returned to the car. Just in case, she thought. Coming here might be the second most stupid thing I've ever done.

Cautiously she continued down the road; fast enough not to draw attention from passersby or neighbors, slow enough not to stir up a cloud of dust. Suddenly, movement to her left sent a shock of adrenaline through her body. Her foot jerked up from the accelerator, her head snapped to the left. The whole field was in motion. Paige let out a sudden gasp as a herd of deer, startled by the car, bolted into action.

"Ho!" she exclaimed in a loud exhale. "Don't do that to me."

Only seconds later the last of the herd fled the field, crossed the road behind the car and disappeared into the neglected cornfield. With adrenaline still pumping through her body, Paige drew a deep breath and composed herself enough to continue down the road.

Her legs still quivered as she neared her mother's house. "Damn deer," she said, rubbing her right thigh.

The curve was just as she remembered it, the remnants of an old wire fence still lining the top edge of a drainage ditch that was overgrown with weeds and tall grass. Just past the curve was the boulder, smaller, though, than she remembered, marking the corner of the driveway. A large rusty mailbox, atop a wooden post, marked the other side.

Paige slowed the car to a crawl as she looked across a yard of dying grass and flourishing weeds. There were no flowers, only a neglected juniper on either side of the front step to accent the little one-story house. The cardboard was gone from the front bedroom window and someone had replaced the broken glass. No one needs to break in for clothes anymore . . . or out for safety.

Then, something caught her eye. The tires crunched to a stop in the gravel just beyond the driveway. There, beneath the shade of a maple, sat a rusty once-blue bouncy chair. Her next attempt at a deep breath was unsuccessful. Acids churned in her stomach and threatened to rise.

She could see him there, as clearly as sixteen years ago, in his faded jeans and his favorite NBPD T-shirt. He was leaning forward, his forearms resting on his knees, as he so often did, a cigarette held loosely between yellowed fingers. His thoughts were his own; the process that formed them a mystery. All Paige knew was that the number of beer cans sitting on the metal TV tray next to the chair determined when those thoughts would become action—when her being gone was essential.

The air coming in the open car window carried a sudden whiff of familiarity. The smell of cigarette smoke mixed with perspiration and two-day-old deodorant started the churning in her stomach once again. She hit the button and rolled up the window. Not possible, she reminded herself, just my mind playing nasty tricks. He's gone—forever. The reminder did little to settle her stomach. The discomfort continued while her mind leapt to a disturbing conclusion. She still lives here.

Paige looked more closely at the front of the house and the driveway, searching for another sign that would confirm it. Why wouldn't she still be here? She backed the car enough to pull into the drive. Geri Panning, nerve endings dulled by alcohol, had walked across the coals of hell unscathed. It would be just like her to stay right here.

There was no other car in the driveway. Paige left the old Mazda idling and walked tentatively past the side of the house. She stopped briefly to look through the window of the side door. Not much to see there, a hooded sweatshirt and a flannel jacket that could belong to anyone. She stopped longer at the kitchen window. Her heart felt as though it rolled over in her chest, then resumed its rapid pace. She stared at the center of the small kitchen. They were still there—the brown Formica table with the edge missing on one end, and the mismatched chairs. The same damn table and chairs.

Paige turned from the window quickly before the vision could form fully in her mind. It would always be the last vision she had of him, and just because it was the last made it no better than the rest. She cursed silently as she rounded the back corner of the house. Like so many things from her childhood, the perspective had changed. It was smaller and closer to the house than she remembered, but the barn was still there. Her refuge, her hiding place. She'd dreaded ever seeing it again, but surprisingly the sight of it didn't repulse her.

When she was very young it had frightened her—the spiders and the mice and the cold of winter. But eventually her fears had turned to anger—at him, at her mother, at the unfairness. Other children didn't have the same fears, they didn't have to hide; she knew that, she had been to their homes. It wasn't fair. But she did what she had to do, fair or not. She became better at managing her life, and with that came self-reliance and a strange kind of confidence that replaced some of the anger. She learned to appreciate her hiding place, hold it in her mind as a kind of trophy, a personal triumph he had been unable to deny her. She felt it even now as she continued around to the back of the barn.

A subdivision of houses now occupied old man Bennett's horse pasture; her secret path to and from her hide-out was gone. Gone, too, was her first entrance into the barn. The woodchuck hole that

3

led under the side boards and into an old tool box, that she had widened until she could squeeze through it, was now filled with rocks and concrete. When she glanced up, another stab of adrenaline took her back to her early teens and the climb up the corner of the barn to the loft window. She looked at the open pane with its still-missing glass and marveled. How the hell did I ever do that? Amazing what desperation can do. Bruises and splinters were of little consequence then. They healed and were forgotten in a matter of days. It was avoiding the other pain that mattered most. Up there she couldn't hear the cursing and the yelling; she could never be trapped in the bedroom for a beating, or worse. And, being gone, she finally realized, gave him one less reason to hit her mother. Yes, up there, it was much better.

Her ears, fine tuned to his comings and goings over the years, picked up the sound of a vehicle nearing the curve. At the sound, Paige bolted into a full sprint down the drive. She scrambled into the car and pulled out into the road before the approaching vehicle cleared the curve. With her heart still sprinting, she hit the accelerator and left a cloud of dust rising behind her.

The instinct to flee held strong through the first turn onto Jenkins Road and the second, a mile down, onto Deer Run Lane. It held for two more miles before Paige was able to slow enough to pull the car into an inconspicuous tractor drive at the edge of a field. A giant oak marked the corner of a boundary lined with loosely piled field stones.

There was no one in sight for miles; the closest buildings looked toy-like in the distance. Still, Paige hurried from the car to open the trunk. She pushed the rag partially covering the license plate back into the trunk and felt immediate relief. Forgetting it would have given some cop reason enough to pull her over, and the last thing she wanted to do was give them a cause that she could have controlled.

What control she still had in her life she was determined to hang on to, whatever it cost. Paige lifted the quilted blanket that covered everything she owned, neatly arranged in the trunk of her car, and pulled open her toiletries bag. The cost today would be about a half a bottle of Maalox.

4

Chapter 2

Over the years there had been more than a few hungry hounds sniffing around the possibility of settling with Geri Panning. Although still blue at the collar, they had become less substance dependent and more financially stable in recent years. No coincidence that this corresponded to the length of time Geri had been clean and sober herself. Yet, none of them had the emotional stamina to stay, or the chutzpah to challenge Jack Beaman, North Branch's most respected detective. Bob Denby was no exception.

He closed the customer door to the auto shop that bore his name and secured the padlock. He didn't notice the car stopping in the street short of the stop sign, but he recognized the voice before he turned around.

"Long day eh, Bob? You've been closin' up kinda late this week."

He took enough time in turning around to be sure his response to the detective was adequately tempered. He was pretty sure that the fire burning in Jack Beaman's gut had something to do with Geri Panning, but Bob had been around gasoline long enough to know not to shoot sparks at it. He wiped his brow with the cleanest part of his sleeve and replaced his cap as he turned.

"Haven't been able to replace Dave yet. People need their cars. One way or the other the work's gotta get done."

"That's exactly why folks keep bringin' their cars to you," Jack returned. "That kinda reputation is a gold-plated business card. Too bad about Dave—sometimes those old warrants get past us, especially when people move around. I just happened to catch that one. Well, I just wanted to see how you were doing." He raised his hand and started ahead as if to leave, then stopped. "Oh, hey, I almost forgot. You probably already know, there have been those rumors around town about that other mechanic of yours. Folks sayin' that he was seen buying crack in the red-light district. Might be nothing, but I'd keep my eye on him if I was you." He raised his hand once more. "Well, you take care now. I'll keep my ears open for another mechanic." He kept his focus on the grease-marked face of Bob Denby for a few seconds longer, then slowly pulled away.

It wasn't harassment, Jack had convinced himself, merely a good example of micro-enforcement. Not that Bob Denby's oxygen-starved brain hadn't tried to make a case for harassment. He had, in the beginning, when those pesky code violations were noticed, and the IRS called for an audit. It's just a damn shame that he can't get clear of the carbon dioxide fumes long enough to understand the difference. Jack Beaman snickered to himself. "Someday, guys like that are gonna learn that they can't rub up against *my* people unless they squeak," he muttered. "And Geri Panning *is* my people, no matter what the reason, and interference by anyone, even poor ol' Bob, just won't be tolerated. Ol' Jack won't even tolerate soap scum."

Jack pulled into the parking lot of his daughter's apartment complex and parked next to the two-year-old Civic he had bought her. The first foreign car he had ever purchased. He had endured the riding from the guys at the station and defended his major flip-flop the best he could. His own father would have set it aflame if he were alive. For him, Pearl Harbor was an unforgivable sin, and Jack grew up with daily reminders of it. Even now, as he looked at the little silver car, it seemed as though someone else must have bought it. How his mind had gotten from there to here he couldn't even say. He always had to go back to his list: it had been assembled right here in the US by blue-collar

Americans (he had made sure), it got great fuel economy in the city (important for a single mother with no child support), it ranked very high for reliability by *Consumer Report*, and it was as safe a small car as he could find. And the whole process of American-made cars had been bastardized anyway. *That* was why it was sitting there in his daughter's parking space.

Jackie Beaman met her father at the door of her first-floor apartment and hugged him graciously. "I hope you're ready for this," she warned. "There's a wired three-year-old in there too excited to take his nap because his Popu was coming."

Jack chuckled and kissed her on the cheek. "I don't know what it is—probably that I know that I only have him for a short time—but it's magical how much energy I have around him. I don't feel tired at all until he's gone."

"Well, he loves you and can't wait to go to your house. And you know how much I appreciate you taking him. Sister or not, I can't expect Rachael to watch him on Friday night when she has him most of the week. Danny and I really need some time alone if we're going to make this thing work."

Before Jack could say another word, the bathroom door burst open and with a loud "Popu," Bradley Beaman struggled to run toward him.

"Hey, little buddy," Jack managed without laughing, "you gotta pull them pants *up* if you expect to do any running."

He bent down, pulled the Spiderman pants up over the tiny buttocks and lifted his grandson into his arms. "You and Popu gonna have a good time tonight?"

Bradley nodded his head vigorously and squeezed his arms around his grandfather's neck.

"Yeah, we'll have fun," Jack said with a wink at Jackie. "Let's get your britches on and grab your bag and get the heck outta Dodge, okay?"

Jackie wiggled a pair of jeans over Bradley's legs as Jack held him, and snapped them in place.

"Where are you two going tonight?" Jack asked.

"I don't know," she returned. "I couldn't get him to commit to anything specific. Just some *free time* as he calls it."

7

"Make him take you someplace nice. It won't hurt him to spend a little money on you."

"It's not about money, Dad. You know better than that." She picked up Bradley's essentials bag and hung it over her father's free shoulder. "It's about getting a little relief from job stress and the demands of even the cutest little bug on earth." She brushed dark brown hair the color of her own from Bradley's forehead. "I'm going to do everything I can to make this work."

It was too much talk and not a quick enough exit for Bradley. He clamped his hand over his grandfather's mustache. "Okay," Jack said as he removed it gently, "we're on our way." His last words were directed at his daughter. "Just make sure Danny Boy is meeting you halfway."

Chapter 3

Paige passed the Baker Road exit on I-94, her mind made up to keep pushing east. Her stomach tightened at the thought of the long security lines at the bridge, but crossing from Detroit into Windsor was still the best choice for leaving the country. She'd had three states and 1,100 miles to think about it and it seemed the only answer to ease the nagging vulnerability that had returned with a vengeance after the stop at her mother's house. Maybe it was nothing to worry about. She had tried for days to convince herself of it. But she hadn't stayed free for sixteen years by ignoring her instincts.

There was no way of knowing if she ever could have stopped safely—experienced familiarity, grown accustomed to her surroundings. Maybe it had been possible—in some pretty little town, with a job that could have been a career, in a real house and a real relationship. Maybe it could have been a big city like Denver where she could have blended into a blue-denim society down under the radar. Or that little town in Washington, the one with the old courthouse and its clock tower overlooking the park right in the middle of town. The picture was clear, but the name had escaped her. When was it? Long after she and Derrick had run to California. Was it two years after San Francisco, after Derrick died? Three years? She didn't want to think about Derrick, not now. It was too hard to think past the gaunt, disease-ridden creature that he had become to see how sparkling blue his eyes were with the ocean at his back. And it had been years since she had been able to remember the sound of his laughter. All she could remember was that the sound of it made her feel as if there was no fear it couldn't ease and no event, no matter how potentially devastating, that it couldn't shrink into obscurity. And that wasn't enough to hold her thoughts in a happy place. There had been too much sadness and too much time.

No, she wouldn't think about him now. She forced her eyes from the road as she forced the thoughts of him from her mind. The gas gauge read below an eighth of a tank, lower than her rule of the road: start looking for a good gas price at a quarter of a tank. Too late for that; she took the next exit

How nice it would be to be coming home, pulling into somewhere pretty, like that little town in Washington with the name that eludes me. I'd fill up at a station like this one, Paige thought as she emerged from the car and stretched her back, and be ready for the work week. She lifted the pump handle and settled the nozzle in place. As she reached for the window squeegee between the pumps she caught a glimpse of the woman on the other side. With a graceful bend at the waist and long dark hair falling over her shoulder, she brought the Washington memory back clear and full.

It had begun on a day like this, sunny and warm, spending her lunchtime eating a deli sandwich in the park and listening to the woman with the licorice-colored hair she had met there tell her how ants actually open the peony buds, and wondering how long it would take before they made love.

It hadn't taken long, really, three or four days if her memory was accurate, before Audrey was in her arms. Audrey Graves, one of the few women whose name and face had imprinted on her memory. One of the few whose eyes had held hope, whose tears she hadn't been able to avoid.

The whole encounter was supposed to be easy, uncomplicated—days full of anticipation, nights full of passion. No promises, no regrets. And at first it was just that. They would

10

meet at lunch and tease each other with talk of flowers and movies and books they'd read. And as they talked, their eyes would twinkle with remembrance of the night before and lay a sizzling path of anticipation for the night to come. She should have known that it was too good to be true the first time she woke with the sun shining warm and bright and Audrey was still in her arms and the voice in her head that always spoke its warning was silent. In its place was a harmony of murmurs and whispers, and the sounds made her smile. She should have known when the world held still and Audrey returned her smile and closed her eyes, and there was no need to rush into frenzied love-making. She should have known then.

And maybe she did, unconsciously. Maybe she just wanted to believe that it was all right, to fall in love, just that once. That somehow, magically, the past would be forgotten—forgiven—and that the sublime was possible, even deserved. After all, didn't everyone have dreams, and the hope that one day those dreams would be fulfilled? Wasn't that what kept life worth living? Sure it was—if you were anyone but Paige Flemming, with a past that would sooner or later destroy any and every love relationship no matter how much in love you were.

The lesson wasn't an easy one to learn. She was a survivor. She had learned to adapt, physically and emotionally, to find the good in the tiniest and most commonly overlooked things in life. And hope—that life would be easier, happier, safer—was an essential molecule of survival. To disavow that hope proved to be an even harder task than making it through the tough times.

Periodically, hope would lift its head high, smile broadly, and breathe deeply, like during her time with Audrey and with Moni. Each time she would have to force it back down and hold it like you would a fully inflated ball beneath the surface of the water. The effort it took would eventually wear her out. Someday, she figured, either the ball would lose its air and any thoughts of a relationship like her good friends Moni and Katherine had would be gone for good, or she'd give in, take the path of least resistance, and enjoy a relationship for as long as she could. But she knew how high a risk that was and how unfair it would be to someone else. So for now, and for as long as she could, she'd hold the ball down. And for a couple of days she would enjoy someone else's relationship.

Paige pulled off at the next exit, crossed the bridge over I-94 and re-entered the highway heading west. She pulled the cell phone from her waistband and called Moni.

Chapter 4

"You're sure you don't mind not having any notice?" Paige asked at the release of a long hug from Moni.

"No, I should thank you," Moni returned with a grin. "Your call brought a halt to an argument that had been going on far too long."

"If you ever realize how lucky you are, you'd never argue."

She led Paige to the living room of the Cape Cod–style cottage and replied, "That thought is exactly why our first argument was so hard for me to understand. I kept saying that I was sorry afterwards and that we'd never argue again. But older and wiser isn't just a cliché. Katherine was right when she said that we would argue again, probably many times, and that we would just have to learn to do it constructively."

"So, have you?" Paige asked, settling on the butter-rich feel of a mustard-colored leather couch.

"I think it's a process. We're getting better at it."

Better at arguing? Paige stared at Moni. How is that possible? Arguments aren't debates. They're stands based on emotion, fanned by anger—confrontations that, if not walked away from, always escalate into violence. That was a fact she knew well. What Moni was talking about, she had no idea. Finally, she asked, "What did you disagree on?"

"Oh," Moni flipped her hand in dismissal, "something stupid.

13

No, I guess it isn't stupid if it leads to an argument. Can I get you something to drink?"

"Just ice water."

When she returned from the kitchen, Moni continued her explanation. "I agreed to do an art display for a school board function at the high school where I teach which I thought would bring more community awareness to our art department. But the timing is shitty. We've been without a contract all year—in fact, it looks like we'll finish the year without one—and the union has us withholding all non-contractual services. Katherine's really upset with me. Both the media center and the music department turned down the project, but I rationalized that I wouldn't be doing it on school time and it's not in the building, and maybe it would give me some points when it comes to budget cuts and eliminating programs."

"What's wrong with watching out for yourself?"

"School contract negotiations are only successful through solidarity. Katherine's been through many negotiation processes, when she taught both at the high school level and at the college level where she is now, and she sees this as a breach of that solidarity."

Paige frowned, one eyebrow scrunched higher than the other. "So, if they cut out your art classes would the music teacher step up and tell them to take half of her classes in order to save half of yours?"

Moni smiled and shook her head. "No, I'm sure she wouldn't."

"Then it's only solidarity when it affects everyone."

"*You* should be arguing this one with Katherine," Moni replied with a look of exasperation.

Paige held up a hand. "Oh, no. I make it a practice not to ruffle the feathers of a hostess." She frowned again. "I didn't already, did I? Are you sure she doesn't mind me showing up like this?"

"No, Paige. Stop worrying. She went to the store for some groceries. Katherine really likes you. In fact," Moni held up her index finger and disappeared into an adjoining room. She returned quickly with a manila envelope. "I found this great

14

crossword and sealed it up, and she's been very anxious to challenge you with it."

"She doesn't think that I can beat her, does she?"

Moni shrugged. "I don't know . . . last time she only beat you by three words. That constitutes at least a healthy respect. I'll lose quick money if it's not the first thing she talks about when she gets in the door. End of the week—no work tomorrow—she'll want to challenge you tonight. Are you still a night cat, or would you rather make her wait until tomorrow?"

"I'd have been on the road all night, but . . ."

Moni made eye contact and held it for a moment before saying, "Canada. You're nervous again."

There had only been two people in her life who knew her this well, and Derrick was gone. How *he* knew what he knew was no surprise. They'd run together, drank together, cursed life's circumstances then laughed in the face of them. They'd shared the tears in the middle of the night and understood the fears that brought them. But Moni . . . it was never clear how she knew what she knew. It couldn't have come from one night of sexual intimacy or one night of confession. How did she know so much more than anyone else from just playing ball and working crosswords and dancing? It had always been a quandary, yet asking never seemed appropriate. Someday, she promised, someday.

"I'm sorry," Moni was saying. "I shouldn't make assumptions. It's really—"

"I saw a show on television," Paige started. "Almost two weeks ago. Anyway, the main character takes murder cases from the cold case files and tries to solve them. I wasn't going to watch it, but I turned back to it. I couldn't help it." She finally pulled her eyes from a distant stare to look at Moni. "Do you know how that is?"

Moni nodded silently.

Paige continued. "It was such a good show that I was drawn in right away. A college boy had been murdered in an alley outside a gay bar in 1964—before Stonewall—when raids and harassment and beatings by the police were as prevalent as those by citizens.

Gay-bashing and hate crimes didn't exist according to the law, so it wasn't a surprise that the police didn't try very hard to solve the boy's murder."

She hadn't meant to tell the story, but Moni was listening so intently that Paige decided to continue. "So, this woman investigator and her team tracked down family and friends and witnesses, and thirty years after the incident they questioned them. She found out that there had been a violent police raid that same night, and that the boy and his lover had been harassed by some neighborhood thugs earlier in the evening. The question was, did the thugs wait for him to come out of the bar and kill him, or did the police kill him in the raid?"

Paige took a long drink of the ice water that had sat untouched in front of her. "All through the show they kept flashing back during scenes and showing the characters as they looked in 1964, and the street and the buildings—it was really effective."

"So, who did it?" Moni asked.

Paige smiled at her impatience. "They interviewed the retired cop who had been a rookie when he wrote up the harassment incident. He had been in on the raid as well. He admitted that he and his partner had seen the thugs beating the boy in the alley after the raid but had looked the other way and not reported it. He claimed that he was too ashamed to come forward and testify later. The breakthrough was when he showed a picture of his gay son and his lover and said that he always wanted his son to think that he was a good guy. The investigator said, 'Then be that good guy for him now.'"

"And he did," Moni concluded, "because it hit home."

Paige nodded. "Thirty years later and they caught all three of the guys involved."

"And then you put yourself in their place."

"It was a short step . . . I headed out of there the next morning."

"Paige, maybe you should consider—"

"No."

Katherine, in a pair of cut-off sweats and an over-sized sweat-shirt, was settled against the end of the couch with her favorite dictionary and a clipboard resting against upright thighs.

Paige had chosen the floor. She lay stretched on her stomach, across the end of the area rug, with a clipboard and a dog-eared crossword dictionary in front of her. Halfway through the puzzle she was finding it hard to concentrate. Moni had retired to the guestroom hours ago to watch television, so there was no other presence, no distractions, nothing but soft jazz playing in the background. But her own thoughts kept interrupting her concentration, weakening whatever natural competitiveness she had.

It was nothing new—self-doubt had plagued her for as long as she could remember. The times when she was on the dance floor or diving for a ball in the outfield, self-doubt was unwarranted and more easily overcome. But other times, like this—well, no matter how many puzzles she had solved, a high-school dropout has no business challenging a college professor to anything involving words.

This is going to be embarrassing, and drinking enough to negate it isn't an option here. So, concentrate then. At least make a good showing.

She focused again on forty down. Dancer/choreographer. *Annie Get Your Gun* and *Showboat*. First president of the American Dance Association. Third letter "M", last letter "S".

How did this start in the first place? It wasn't an impulse challenge fueled by alcohol, although there had been more of them than she cared to admit. Claiming that you can ride a Harley for the first time while you're drunk isn't a wise choice. Separating the steps from the coach's back porch with it certainly doesn't substantiate prowess. Nor does jumping from a high-diving board when the dog-paddle is your best stroke.

No, this challenge was not of her own making. She would not have made it sober and she would not allow herself any more than a social drink around Katherine. It was bad enough that Moni had been witness to more than a few party nights. It would be nice to be able to prove that those days were behind her.

Oh, well, it doesn't matter how it got started, what matters now is not looking like the uneducated fool that I am. Come on, concentrate.

Suddenly, there it was. Tamiris. Yes! It fits and that makes forty-five across Rainey. Yep, Mother of the Blues. Beautiful.

"Okay, break time," Moni announced as she entered the room. "I've had enough alone time for a while." Then she burst into laughter at the sight of the large black-and-white cat, paws curled beneath her, perched contently on the small of Paige's back. "How long has she been there?"

"Too long," Paige returned, her head resting on folded arms.

"A huge compliment," Katherine said, gently brushing a mostly black long hair from beneath her knees. "Miss Social Recluse is usually nowhere to be found until any company has left the premises."

"Come on, Bitty Boo," Moni coaxed.

But the cat ignored her and like a champion log-roller stayed atop Paige's body as she rolled slowing onto her back.

"Just push her off, Paige," Moni said. "She won't bite."

Paige raised her knees and settled on her back. "She's fine," she said, her caresses answered with loud purring. "I'd never kick a lady off my lap."

Katherine laughed softly. "I'm sure that's the first time she's been called *that*."

"She's our Princess and the Pea," explained Moni. "Okay, you two go get something to drink. I'm curious to see where you are."

Paige placed Bitty on the chair and followed Katherine into the kitchen.

Moni unfolded the page of the completed puzzle from her pocket and compared it first to Katherine's and then to Paige's. "Oh, this will be good."

"Paige, when are you going to take me up on my offer of computer lessons?" Katherine asked. "I'm serious. The more skills you have on the computer, the more job opportunities are out there for you . . . and the lessons are free," she added with a smile.

"I've picked up a little bit on my own. It's not that I don't appreciate the offer, Katherine, it's just that the better jobs will expect me to stay longer than I want."

"Are you so sure that it would be a mistake?"

Paige finished a bite of Danish before answering. "I've grappled with that decision all my life it seems."

"And the decision always goes the same way," Katherine added.

Paige nodded. "And I'm still free."

"I know that it's easy for someone else to think that there are better possibilities for you, but you're a smart woman and I know you could be doing better for yourself."

"Street smart," Paige added.

"Smart is smart; it doesn't matter how you got that way."

"It matters *why*."

"You two giving up the challenge for tonight?" Moni asked as she entered the kitchen with both cats at her heels.

Katherine looked to Paige and replied, "I'd only lie awake all night thinking about it."

"Let's go then." Paige rose from the table, picked up the last of her Danish in a napkin and headed for the living room.

They mean well. I know that they just want me to be happy, to have a good life. Paige settled again on the floor and began the process needed to clear her mind and concentrate on the puzzle. What they can't understand is that I am happy. It's a relative thing. Nobody gives it to you; you find it for yourself. You do what you have to do to keep yourself safe and fed. Nobody's going to do that for you, either. And if you keep life simple, it doesn't take much to make you happy. Today, happiness is not making a fool out of myself. So, clear away the unnecessary and focus.

It was after three A.M. when a sleepy-eyed Moni emerged from the guestroom and curled herself into a chair with a cup of coffee. Out of respect for the effort being put into the challenge she resisted the temptation to check their progress. Neither Paige nor Katherine looked up.

Moni sipped her coffee and watched. She had chosen the puzzle because it included the accomplishments of women and because it was rated as difficult. But it's hard to judge how difficult it is when you're staring at the answers.

She hadn't anticipated that it would take this long. Her own experience with puzzles was limited to working some with Paige years ago and a few with Katherine. Working one alone, however, and one evidently this difficult, was a whole different thing.

She also hadn't anticipated how much she wanted Paige to win this challenge. At first it seemed to be the good old American "pulling for the underdog" thing—the college professor versus the high school drop-out who works crossword puzzles every day to improve her vocabulary. But as the hours passed and she thought about it more, she realized that it was more personal than that. Paige was more than an underdog, she was vulnerable deep inside where you had to look real hard to know—a personal question of worth covered with layers of self-reliance and irreverence. It was why she drank and why she danced, and why she never backed down from a challenge.

And there was another reason for wanting Paige to win—a selfish one: she had been Moni's first lover. Winning, or at least a good showing, was a kind of validation. Validation that Paige was worthy of her love, deserving of her loyalty and her forgiveness, and that despite her age, Moni had made a good choice. Selfish, no doubt. She hoped Katherine would understand.

Moni looked from one to the other, both women so closed in their concentration. They'd been neck and neck hours earlier, but there was no way of knowing what could have stumped one or both of them since. Moni quietly looked at the answers again and waited anxiously.

Minutes later, Katherine shifted and sat upright. Paige quickly erased something and hurriedly filled in the squares again. More movement than Moni had seen in hours. She watched Paige check the bottom of the page, then lift her head and smile. She looked over at Moni, but before she could say anything Katherine's voice rang out.

"Done."

Immediately Paige collapsed face down on the rug. Arms stretched above her head, she muttered something indiscernible.

Moni jumped up from the chair. "You had it," she directed at Paige, "didn't you? Why didn't you say it?"

Paige muttered into the rug, but didn't move.

"Here, Moni." Katherine handed her the puzzle. "I know you're itching to check our answers." She knelt beside Paige and kneaded her shoulders. "Hey, are you as stiff as I am?"

Paige turned her head to the side. "That would be a yes."

"Let's all go for a walk," she said, offering Paige a hand up. "We've earned it."

"Don't you want to know?" Moni asked, following them out the door.

"The look on your face said it all," Katherine replied. She turned and placed a kiss on Moni's cheek. "Paige had me; she just didn't believe it in time."

Chapter 5

Three o'clock on Tuesdays and Thursdays at Grainger's Mid-Town Grill was always slow. Which meant that the service was prompt, the food was hot, and Jack could always count on sitting at his favorite booth. It was, of course, in Geri Panning's section and, since business was slow, she always had time to sit and talk with him. An extra break now and then was not a concern; after all, what boss would fire her for talking with North Branch's chief detective? The visits had become a weekly ritual.

"So," Jack began as Geri sat down across from him, "tell me about that movie you saw last week."

"Oh, yeah. I did want to see that one," she said. "I tried to get Gretchen to go with me, but she's got too much going on with that kid of hers." Geri shook her head. "Almost thirty and I don't think he's worked three weeks of it at one stretch. Anyway, I guess I wasn't up to going by myself."

"That boyfriend of yours too cheap to take you to the movies?"

"No, that ain't it." She sipped her coffee, then stared blankly out the large window.

Jack waited as if what she was hesitant to say was news to him.

Geri turned back to her coffee, running her finger around the rim of the cup. "Bob ain't been coming around for a while now."

"Well hell, honey, it don't seem like the boy's naturally right. There's gotta be something wrong with a man that can't appreciate a lady like you."

Geri tucked back a wayward sprig of gray-streaked blondish hair too short for her ponytail. "He was busy, or tired, working long hours at the shop, or he forgot to call. I've been around long enough to get the message. He didn't have to say it."

"I'm sorry, Geri," he said as he placed his hand over hers on the table.

"I'm okay," she said with a look of resolve. "It ain't enough for me to trade this coffee in on a seven 'n seven. I was kinda hoping he'd be celebrating with me next week, though. Seven years' sobriety," she said with a tip of her head. "Kinda wanted to celebrate, with somebody other than my sponsor."

"Then, we will," he said, squeezing her hand. "You name it—and I'm sparing no cost. We'll have a hell of a celebration."

She pulled her hand from under his. "Hey, I don't need no sympathy celebration. I've had enough of them to make it through my next two lives."

"No sympathy being offered. I'm just real proud of you, Geri, that's all. It's fitting that you have someone to celebrate something like this with."

The sharp blue eyes only stared back at him. Like so many times before, he expected her to get up without a word and leave him sitting there. A reaction he thought he understood. He had been pretty relentless during the investigation of her husband's murder. But he had only been doing his job, she had to understand that. The years had to have healed that wound. Besides, it wasn't her he was after.

He looked up from his coffee, surprised that she was still staring at him. "I got ketchup on my face or something?" he asked. He ran a napkin over his mouth.

"A man like you coming in here botherin' with me has got to be a lonely man."

"Nah," he replied with a shake of his head. "Oh, I don't deny that I was pretty lonely a good while after my wife died, but I got plenty to keep me busy. I just thought you'd appreciate me taking you out proper like you ought to be. Someday I'm really gonna believe that you don't want to go out with me."

"A really nice place to eat?"

Finally. He responded with a smile that lifted the ends of his mustache into a straight line. "The Heritage House."

She stood, a noticeable red tinge coloring her thin cheeks. The harsh lines of her smile softened and she smoothed the front of her black uniform pants. "I'll go buy me something nice to wear this weekend. Been a while since I needed something nice." She picked up her cup and the last of Jack's dishes. "I'll be back with a fresh cup of coffee for you."

"Hey, that'll be perfect."

The station was buzzing with more than the usual amount of activity when Jack returned from lunch.

"How many hurt, Bill? I caught the call on my radio as I was pulling in."

"Don't know for sure yet," the desk sergeant replied. "One's critical."

Jack scowled. "What the hell's anybody doing passing a stopped school bus anyway?"

"Some guy on a motorcycle."

"We need to start doing some serious educating," Jack returned, "and handing out some hefty fines. There's too much of that crap going on—not pulling over for ambulances, turning in front of fire trucks. Let me know when you find out who this moron is."

"Yep."

Jack muttered his way back to his desk. Like every other officer he knew, it was seeing the kids hurt that got to him the most. Domestic violence was no apple pie either, but women, he figured, at least had a choice.

He pulled an old folder from the bottom drawer and rolled his chair back to use the drawer as a footstool.

"Okay," he said aloud, "I underestimated you." As he had done numerous times over the years, he began to read through the list of juvenile offenses—truancies, a lot of them, B & E's, petty

24

larceny—for his most elusive nemesis. "How did you do it? How did a sixteen-year-old juvenile delinquent just disappear on me?" He stared at the name on the file, Ann Panning, a name he had entered into system after system and state after state. And got nothing in return. There was no such person. And the face—too young, too much like a hundred other eleven-year-olds across the country. And a computer-aged image that may be too far off the mark to be useful. What kind of a parent doesn't have pictures of their kids, lots of them, every year, every event? Pictures of them being silly, being children, growing up. He could understand no graduation picture since she never graduated. But only *one* lousy picture?

He pushed the photo back under the clip. This is all Geri Panning could come up with? I don't get it. Not yet anyway. But I will. And when I do, I'll find you, Ann Panning—whether you're dead or alive or incarcerated, I'll find you or I'll go to my grave tryin'.

Chapter 6

It was one of the most peaceful Saturday mornings Paige could remember. Actually, it was twelve-thirty, but it still felt like morning. A hushed breeze blew late spring–scented puffs across the deck where Paige sat alone. The sun was quickly chasing away the morning chill that had made a sweatshirt necessary and now bathed her face in warmth.

She lifted her head from the back of the deck chair and opened her eyes to the bright green of Moni and Katherine's backyard. Lush woods of maples and pines ran along the back and west side, while a wooden privacy fence, partially covered with morning glory vines and clematis, bordered the east. It was beautiful. Another example, she mused, of a God she wasn't sure existed giving her glimpses of a heaven she'd never see. Paige inhaled a deep, full breath of the freshness and whispered to Bitty as she settled onto her lap, "I could stay here forever."

The wish was given its freedom to linger, to play out its fantasy without rebuke. And in the space of a long sip of coffee, the house on the other side of the fence was for sale and the salary from her new job qualified her for a zero-down loan. Paige had cats of her own, cuddling with her and counting on her, and she had a lover and good friends next door, and the closest thing to a family that she had ever imagined. In that short space of time, life—her life—had become perfect. For that moment, and for as long as the fantasy lasted, normalcy, the expected, was real, as real as a Robert Louis Stevenson moment could make it.

There was a deck on her house, too, and lawn chairs and a grill with a side burner. And she'd protect everything with covers in the winter and uncover them early every spring. She'd plant perennials like crocuses and gladioli and she'd remember right where they would be coming up and she'd watch for them. It wouldn't matter that the lawn needed mowing on her only day off, or if she had to shovel four inches of overnight snow off the drive before she went to work. She would clean the gutters faithfully every fall and wash the windows every spring.

A moment later, however, her ideal life was gone when the ball of purring black-and-white fur jumped from her lap at the sight of a pair of chickadees landing on a feeder just out of squirrel range from the deck. Wishes and dreams, she knew, couldn't be expected to last long—the weight of a lifetime cannot be carried on butterfly wings.

So, resolute, Paige settled for watching Bitty as she inched forward in the grass, lowered her haunches and waited. Her eyes locked unflinchingly on her prey as if that would hold them there until she was within striking distance. She inched closer and stopped, settling momentarily into a non-threatening posture. Her eyes still held her prey captive as the little birds fluttered and fed unaware. Finally, Bitty chanced a long slinky move forward and stopped low on her haunches as the birds' heads came up.

Another foot, Paige figured, but then what? A leap over a baffle that even the most acrobatic squirrel couldn't clear? Yet, you try every day, don't you? Get as close as you can, some days closer than others, but never capture a single bird. Or have you, sometime in the past, taken your prey unaware from a low bush, and known the reality of it? Is that what keeps you trying? Is that what throws off the frustration of failure and improbability and feeds the possibility? The fact that it was once possible? And what if you couldn't try every day, what then? Feline depression, little reason left to eat or play or purr?

Not a worry today, though, Bitty was focused and intent. She raised her haunches once more and sprang quickly for the pole. But, as must have happened countless times before, the birds were quicker and higher, leaving Bitty to leap futilely at them as they left the feeder. Head up, Bitty chased the fleeting forms, maybe out of frustration or maybe out of pure determination, all the way across the yard until they disappeared beyond the fence and high into a tree. She took her time returning to the deck and took a long drink of water from the dish by the door before jumping back onto Paige's lap.

"Yeah, it's nothing to be embarrassed about, little girl. It was a gallant attempt." Paige began stroking the long soft fur. "Maybe tomorrow, eh?" The purring began again softly. "Yeah, as long as there's tomorrow."

The glass door slid open and Moni leaned through the opening. "Hey, thanks for making coffee." She smiled brightly. "I see your pal is being a good hostess. Did she sleep with you last night?"

"Oh, yeah, after she licked away all remaining evidence of soap from my face and neck. She curled up against my belly under the covers and purred me to sleep."

"I think she's adopted you. And since it hasn't happened before, I can't tell you what that means. Bring the princess with you," Moni said with a smile. "We're making brunch."

"I just realized something," Moni said as she placed the last of the dishes in the dishwasher. She turned to the table where Paige remained with Katherine. "I haven't seen you smoke since you've been here."

"I quit," Paige replied. "Cold turkey this time. Threw out my last pack of cigarettes just over five months ago."

"No patch or anything?" asked Katherine.

Paige shook her head. "Nothing except poverty and a persistent cough spurring my determination."

Katherine raised her eyebrows. "I'd say that's a pretty good incentive."

Moni high-fived Paige and reclaimed her seat. "And the cough is gone; your lungs have already started to clear themselves. Good for you."

Paige smiled. "I don't even remember when all food started tasting like the bottom of a bird cage. But now that it doesn't anymore I have to be careful—*everything* tastes good." She cupped her hands under her breasts and lifted. "I refuse to strap these moo-moos down with anything but a sports bra anymore, so I don't dare gain any more weight."

Moni laughed, but the flush of her face betrayed a discomfiture Paige that recognized immediately. A complimentary embarrassment was the best definition Paige could come up with. They're attracted to you—the way you look, or move, or the way you look at them—but they're at a loss as to what to do about it. There was a time when she played that for all it was worth, sometimes subtly and sometimes not so subtly. There were also times when alcohol made decisions for her and there was no intent at all. Poor Moni was front and center during one of those times, a striptease that had Paige down to a black lace bra and a team goading Moni to pull the zipper tab of her jeans down with her teeth. Her eyes betrayed her that time. Even through the haze of alcohol Paige recognized it. What she saw there changed the rules of the game from that point on.

". . . then you tell *us*," Katherine was saying, "what you want to do tonight. A smoke-filled bar probably isn't the best choice for avoiding temptation."

"Actually," Paige added a smile, "that's not when I'm most tempted. But I *would* prefer to just enjoy the company of two good friends—maybe someplace nice where I can buy you dinner."

"You just keep getting more mellow every time we see you," Moni said.

"Like fine wine?" Her eyes twinkled with her smile. "Older and wiser? Pick a cliché."

Moni answered quickly, "Oh, it's more than a cliché. I think we're getting to know the real you."

"How about Applebee's in Ann Arbor?" Katherine asked. "Moni?"

"Not too expensive, not too noisy. It's perfect, Katherine. And how about taking the afternoon and walking the nature trail back to the lake?" Moni motioned to Bitty, who had made her way back onto Paige's lap. "Your little pal can come with us. She walks the trail like a dog."

Chapter 7

"Popu, Popu," Bradley's voice bounced with him down the carpeted ramp in the middle of the mall. Jack rose from the bench and lifted his grandson high in the air. He held him above him momentarily and welcomed the excited smile.

"Hey, how's my best pal?" he asked, lowering Bradley into his arms. "Gonna help Popu shop?"

Bradley nodded vigorously and looked toward his mother.

Jackie smiled. "Yep, he's going to be a big boy and help us shop and then we're going to K-Mart so he can spend the birthday money you gave him last week."

"All right, that's what it's there for." Jack rubbed his mustache over Bradley's nose to make him laugh. "You can show Popu what you want and I'll bet that birthday money'll be just right."

"Dad, that's more than enough money to find something he'll like. You're not adding any more to it . . . Now, what kind of present are you looking for?"

"Oh, honey, I have no idea. That's why I'm sitting here in the middle of the mall waiting for you. Help me find something appropriate for a woman who's celebrating seven years of sobriety."

"Is this a new girlfriend, a colleague, what?" she asked.

"Ah, I don't know, someone I've known forever it seems. Sorta had a crush on her in high school, but we hung out in different crowds. She's had a tough life—you know, that case, her husband was killed in her kitchen."

"Oh, *that* case. You're never going to let that go are you, Dad? You know you're bordering on obsession here."

"Now see, that's why I haven't said anything about it for a long time. Even guys I work with would've given it up years ago. They figure she's either in jail somewhere for something else, or dead."

"The daughter of this woman that you're about to buy a present for?" Jackie sent him a perplexing look. "I should try to understand this, but I'm not sure I want to."

He placed Bradley on the floor and took his hand. "I like the lady. That's not so hard to understand."

"That's all this is about? Are you so sure that *she* didn't kill her husband?"

"Every shred of evidence there is points to the daughter," he said, following Bradley's lead toward the ramp. "Besides, Geri passed the poly."

"Okay, you know what? I'm going to let you think I'm swallowing this for now so that we can get this present and I can get home before Danny does. But, someday I'm going to call you on this obsession."

"I have to say, Geri," Jack began, pushing her chair in and seating himself across the table. "Seeing you in that dress takes me back a lot of years."

Geri smoothed a linen napkin over the lap of her new blue dress. "It's not too young looking, is it? I don't want to be one of those women pretending the world can't count the years on my face."

"As they can on mine," he returned. "But that don't mean we can't look damn good for our age. And you sure do tonight."

The smile on her face told him that he had said exactly the right thing. He followed immediately with, "Do you remember the dance when we were juniors, the football dance after we won the championship?"

Her gaze became distant, her thoughts searching back, remembering. "We thought things were so complicated then," she said.

"But they were really so simple, weren't they?" She acknowledged a subtle smile from Jack. "Everybody wanted a dance with the hero. Even me."

Jack frowned. "Why do you say even you?"

"I didn't exactly fit with your crowd. Sometimes it made me mad." She looked into his eyes. "But I wanted to go to that dance; I wanted to be part of the celebration. My friends wouldn't go, so I went by myself."

"I wasn't too much for dances myself; a bonfire would've done me just fine. But I still remember seeing you standin' there, waitin' in that line to dance with me. And I remember thinking I'm going to ask that girl out no matter what."

"You did? You thought that?"

"I sure did. And the following week you quit school. Never got my chance."

"They let the girls stay in school now." She lowered her eyes from his. "My parents didn't believe in abortion."

"Oh," he said. "Well, yes, they can keep right on going to school." Jack cleared his throat. "I was glad, though, that my Jackie graduated first. The baby put the kibosh on veterinary school, though. I hope she'll get to go back and finish some day."

"Is she your only child?"

"No, no she's our last. Her two older brothers have been married, one of them twice now, and living out of town for some time. Don't see as much of them as I'd like. My other daughter, Rachael, and her husband live here in North Branch. Married a dentist; he makes a good living for them." He took a healthy swallow of coffee and noticed that Geri seemed more at ease. "Sure hope my Jackie can find a good one."

"We never stop worrying about our kids, do we?" she said, more as a statement than a question.

"That's a fact, I'm afraid. Just seems to go with the territory." He smiled, hoping to maintain her comfort. "How many children do you have?"

"Had," she said, this time with her eyes directly on his. "I gave my first baby up for adoption, then lived the next three years not being able to deal with it. I started drinking to get through the day and to be able to sleep at night. I had another baby and it wasn't long before the state took him away from me." Her gaze drifted away into a stare. "When I had Annie I swore that nobody was ever gonna take her away from me." She closed her eyes momentarily, then opened them to look again into Jack's. "I've messed up so many lives. I'm living day by day now to take responsibility for that."

He raised his coffee cup over the center of the table. Geri smiled and raised hers to meet it. "Here's to seven years," he said with a smile, "and many more to come."

"To *today*," she corrected. "Clean and sober."

Jack nodded and sipped his coffee. One day at a time was suddenly more than a phrase. He studied Geri's face, just as he had so many others in his career. She was winning her struggle today and that's all she dared to hope for. Tomorrow she'd begin the struggle again. Damn, it must wear a person out.

The waiter refreshed their coffee and patiently took their orders.

"Do you think a person can ever really make up for things they've done?" Geri asked when they were alone again.

"Well, now see that's a question for a more learned man," he replied. "But, I s'pose that's why we have religions—you know, in case it's not possible, we want to know that a higher being forgives us for it."

"I've admitted to God, to myself, and another the exact nature of my wrongs, and I've made a list of all those I've harmed and I'm willing to make amends to all of them. It's part of recovering," she explained. "But, I don't see any way I can make it up to my kids." A frown formed serious lines from the bridge of her nose. "I guess that's why I understand my friend Gretchen at work, why she keeps trying with her son. She don't want any regrets, you know?"

"Uh, huh," he replied without really understanding.

"Did I tell you?" she asked. "He's in trouble again. He hurt some kids with his motorcycle."

"That was Gretchen's son?"

"He just got his license back. Poor Gretchen is just sick about it. She's been at the hospital everyday checking on those kids, while he's at home whining about a broken leg."

"Does he feel bad at all about what he did?"

"I don't know. Gretchen wants to think he does." Geri's expression was contemplative. "Do you think it's ever okay to give up on someone?"

"Now see, you keep asking me these questions . . ." He leaned back in his chair and thought. "Well, let me ask *you* a question. Do you believe there are bad seeds?"

"Like Damien, like a devil-child?"

Jack smiled. "Maybe not quite *that* evil. But when they don't seem to have a conscience. When bailing them out and giving them chance after chance just makes your own life miserable, or worse puts your welfare in jeopardy."

"I don't think he's ever touched Gretchen, but he's cost her a lot of heartache and hard-earned money."

"If he was my kid," Jack said, "he'd be paying for the consequences of his actions on his own. I figure it's my job to teach 'em right from wrong and help give 'em the skills to make good, moral decisions. If they choose not to, then I figure they'd better be ready to handle what comes next." He hesitated long enough for the waiter to deliver their salads, then continued. "Now protection, that's a whole different matter. Don't nobody wanna hurt one of mine."

Geri lifted her fork through her salad a number of times, but didn't begin to eat it. "What if things you done caused the hurtin'?"

He spoke before he thought. "Guess I'd have to be just as tough on myself then."

"That's where I'm at," she replied. "It's the hardest thing about being sober. I got clean, took back my own name, got my life in order, but it doesn't change that. I caused my Annie a lot of hurt and I don't know if I'll ever be able to tell her I'm sorry."

"No amount of hurt can excuse *some* things, Geri. Don't shoulder more than your share, it'll just beat you down." He waited for eye contact. "Okay?"

She nodded unconvincingly.

"Hey," he said brightly, "I was going to save this until after dinner, but I think now's a good time."

Jack produced a small wrapped box and handed it across the table.

The lines of her face softened into a look of childlike surprise. It looked as if she would say something but she just stared at the little lavender box instead.

"Go on," he insisted, "open it."

Geri smiled and carefully removed the tiny bow, and unwrapped the gift. "Ohh," she breathed softly as she opened the velvet jeweler's box. She removed a gold charm of a smiling sun and exclaimed, "It's beautiful, Jack."

"Can't take all the credit," he admitted. "My daughter helped me pick it out. It's supposed to remind you that whatever yesterday or today has been like, the sun's gonna rise for you tomorrow. You can count on that."

She rose, stepped to the other side of the table and leaned down to place a kiss on his cheek. "You're such a nice man, Jack."

His color heightened. "It's been far too long since a woman told me that." He watched her return to her seat, pleased at the happy expression on her face. "I hope we can do this again real soon."

Chapter 8

They wrapped their conversation around dinner and let the baseball game on the big screen and background music fill the lapses. It was the perfect place to be at the end of a good day. Paige listened intently to Katherine's tales of her teenage years in England and her growing desire to come to the United States. She learned of a family intolerance and conditional love that put Katherine an ocean's distance away and left her alone. A similarity to her own life Paige never would have guessed.

"The families we *make* often offer us more love than the ones we are born into," she was saying.

Paige nodded in agreement. "My mother's way of protecting me from my stepfather was to stick a bowl of food out on the back steps for me after he'd fallen asleep. I had to watch so that *I* got it before the animals did. I'm sure if you asked her that she'd say that she loved me." She met Katherine's eyes, and then Moni's. "You two are the closest thing to a family that I have since Derrick died."

"We know that, Paige," Moni replied.

"Did you ever know your father?" asked Katherine.

Paige shook her head. "My mother always told me that he had been killed in a car accident. The older I got, though, the surer I was that I was the result of a drunken encounter and that she didn't even know his name."

"Maybe it's better not to know," Moni offered.

"Why?" asked Katherine.

"Just another chance for disappointment."

"For a long time I wanted to know," Paige began. "Especially after my mother met RJ. It was my fantasy escape, my chance at a normal life. I'd find him and he'd take me to live with him and his family and he'd be so glad that we found each other. But, eventually, I understood the impossibility of it. The fantasy served its purpose for a while, until I had the strength to let it go."

"It's interesting," Katherine observed, "and remarkable, how the human psyche finds its course to survival."

"Yeah, and sometimes it sure ain't pretty," Paige added.

"It doesn't matter," Moni said. "It's getting there that counts."

Paige dropped her eyes. "Sometimes, though," she said, not wanting to let go of the rare opportunity to say the things she could tell no one else, "it feels like I'm starting over every day. Those are the times I realize it won't ever end—I won't ever—"

"What a nice surprise," came a voice approaching their table.

Moni stood to greet a woman Paige had met once before, and one she wasn't likely to forget. This time, though, the rich auburn hair was pulled into a ponytail that lay loosely from her neck. The gray-blue eyes now held the same severity that had replaced the sparkle in Derrick's eyes after his diagnosis. The dancing, lively woman she had met over four years ago now struggled in obvious pain to walk with the aid of a walker.

"Let me get a chair for you," Moni offered, grabbing the back of one nearby.

"No," the woman replied. "I'd rather stand. It's good therapy, and more comfortable than sitting, believe me."

"I must say," Katherine remarked, "you are unbelievable. How dare they tell Marissa Langford to get used to a wheelchair."

Marissa smiled and straightened to release her grip on the walker. "They didn't know how well I understand pain. Once I got to the good pain there was no stopping me."

Moni took Marissa's hand and motioned toward Paige. "Marissa, do you remember our friend Paige? It was a few years ago—"

38

"Yes," Marissa answered quickly, "I remember." She offered a polite smile but nothing further.

Paige's tone was pleasant. "It's nice to see you again."

"Thank you," Marissa replied and immediately switched her focus to Katherine. "This is my first venture into public. My sister and her husband insisted on taking me to dinner."

"How have you stayed sane all these months?" Katherine asked. "I don't believe I've seen you stay still in one place past five minutes."

Marissa's smile was brighter this time. "I may have been in one place, but I sure wasn't still long. I turned that bed into a gym." She shifted her weight uncomfortably and leaned heavily on the walker. "I called my sub way too many times a week to stay involved in my classes, and lately I've been getting everyone in place to work on this year's show."

"Who's going to work with the dancers?" Moni asked.

Marissa's eyes flashed sharply in her direction. "What do you mean?"

Moni looked to Katherine for what she had quickly gathered was much-needed help.

"We just assumed," Katherine explained, "without thinking that it would be a musical dance production."

Marissa's reply was crisp, "It will be," and clear, "I'll be working with the dancers."

"Oh, that's great," Moni declared in an attempt to soften Marissa's indignation. "What's it going to be this year?"

"Come and help us decide," she returned. "It'll be an all-day movie fest. Evan Adams from the drama department will be there. We can always use a consensus of opinion."

Moni looked from one to the other, saw no objection from Katherine or Paige and replied, "What time?"

"Better make it noon or we'll be turning into pumpkins before we decide." She turned the walker and took an obviously painful step away from the table. "Okay, enough therapy. I'm only a masochist until my stomach growls loud enough to draw attention from nearby tables. I'll see you tomorrow."

Once Marissa was safely out of earshot, Moni tried to explain,

"I didn't realize what was going on with her until I opened my big mouth."

"Well, there's no way she's going to be working with dancers," Paige offered. "Not anytime soon anyway."

"Nine months ago nobody thought she'd be walking, either," Katherine countered.

"But dancing again?" Moni asked

"I know," Katherine said with resolve. "It has to be a hard thing to accept, though."

"Was this from an accident?" asked Paige.

"You would not have believed anyone could have made it out of that mess alive," explained Moni. "The engine of Marissa's car ended up in the front seat beside her."

"Drunk driver?"

"Twice the legal limit," Katherine injected, "and all kinds of priors. Never even slowed down for the light. He should never have been behind the wheel of a car. He'd actually had his license reinstated."

"So did he make it?" Paige asked.

Both Moni and Katherine shook their heads.

"It's usually the other way around."

Moni's tone carried a cynical edge. "Yeah, and the doctors usually put them back together and even if they've killed someone, so many of them end up right back behind the wheel again."

"Not this one," Katherine added. "And maybe not so many in the future if Marissa follows through with legal action against the state. She's hoping that Geoffrey Fieger will take the case."

"I've heard *that* name, even as much as I move around," Paige said. "He defended the suicide doctor."

Moni nodded. "Kevorkian. That case captivated the entire country."

"So, do you really think she has a chance if he takes the case?"

"One thing we've learned from our friend Shayna, the attorney we wanted you to contact, is that if you're going up against big business or the government, the more high profile you are, the better chance you have."

"Splash it all over the media," Paige concluded. Then she

leaned back against the back of her seat and shook her head. "It's so hard to see someone like that . . ."

"It was a shock," Katherine said. "Someone so vital and active and the very next time you see her she's nearly unrecognizable, hooked up to a drip, her body in traction."

"She's made more progress than anyone thought possible," Moni added. "We *are* going to Marissa's tomorrow," she continued, "aren't we?" Her eyes went first to Katherine, who tilted her head and replied, "What would we be saying if we didn't?"

With two pairs of eyes waiting for a response, Paige offered a frown. "You don't need me tagging along. I should get back on the road, anyway."

"Come on, Paige," Moni pleaded. "We've barely had a chance to catch up."

"There will be another day we can spend with Marissa," Katherine directed at Paige. "We're spending tomorrow with you."

"No," Paige moaned, her hand covering her forehead. "That's not . . . you're her friends," she said, regaining her composure. "You already said it, Katherine. What would she think you were saying by not going?"

"Does that mean you will be going with us then?" asked Moni.

"Yeah," Paige replied. "Yeah, I'll go."

Chapter 9

"I've read the screenplays," Marissa explained from the wheel-chair that still provided her with easiest mobility. "But the movie adaptations give me good visuals to decide where my dancers are best suited."

"So with two down, what do you think so far?" Moni asked.

"I know you would love to do *West Side Story*, Evan, but that's way too ambitious for us, for me, this year. I think *Grease* is too. *Footloose* is still a possibility," she handed the box with the last piece of pizza to Katherine, who passed it to Paige, "but I'm leaning toward *Dirty Dancing*."

"It looks to me like you are back in typical 'L' form today," remarked Katherine. "We're well-fed, not too burned out, and," she glanced at her watch, "at six-thirty, we'll get the last one in before the orange tinge sets in."

Marissa smiled and nodded. "Hit it Evan, let's see *Footloose* first, then let Patrick show us his stuff."

"My first observation," Evan began, letting the music continue accompanying the roll of the credits, "is that we have nostalgia and the retro trend going for us whichever way we go."

"You don't think it'll be too overdone by the time November rolls around?" Marissa asked.

"Do you think we can do as vigorous a job of promoting as we did last year?" he asked in return.

Marissa hesitated for a moment before answering, "Yes, we can."

"Then I don't see that there will be a problem," he said, stopping the DVD player and removing the disk. "I do need you to be honest with me as to what you think you can do, though."

Her answer was curt. "I'll be able to do whatever it takes, Evan."

Evan turned to face the three women on the couch. "She's not being bitchy. I hope we all know her well enough to get that."

"I don't need your defense, Evan." Marissa turned her chair sharply and wheeled toward the kitchen. "I'm going to the kitchen if anyone wants anything."

Moni jumped up from the couch and followed her.

Evan dropped his hands from his hips into the pockets of his Levis and nodded as if answering his own thoughts.

"We do understand, Evan," Katherine began. "She's defending her battle and I don't think any of us here are going to judge her for that."

Evan ran his hand through short-cropped hair the color of porcupine quills. "I worry that she has too many battles going at once—her health battle, a legal battle, and trying to keep a job that she absolutely loves."

Katherine's expression matched his concern. "After twelve years," she said, "and all that she has done to build such a respected department, it doesn't seem right that her job should even be in question."

Paige broke her typical silence. "But the job is a physical one, and if she can no longer do it, they have no choice."

"How long is the university giving her?" Katherine asked.

He replied with another brush through his hair. "A year for her teaching position. Maybe they'll keep her as department head, but . . ."

"You're worried about what it will do to her if she can't dance or teach anymore," Paige quickly assumed.

Evan knelt beside the coffee table and spoke in a more intimate tone. "I've known Mar for ten years. She's a fighter in so many ways, but she's never had to face anything like this before." He looked from one woman to the other as though he were searching for reassurance. "I don't know whether to be honest with her about my concern or to follow her lead and just encourage her."

Katherine spoke first. "My instinct would be to support her one hundred percent regardless of your own doubts."

Paige shook her head in disagreement. "Reality's too tough a foe if you're not prepared."

"What did you want to drink?" Moni asked, reaching for the refrigerator door.

Marissa's voice still carried a defensive edge. "I can get it, Moni."

But Moni had the door open and was standing in the way of Marissa's moving the wheelchair close enough to help herself.

"They didn't say so," Moni said as she gathered cans from the refrigerator, "but I'll bet everyone will want something to drink once we get into the movie."

Marissa pulled up a tray from the side of the wheelchair and snapped it into place in front of her. "Put them here," she said. "I don't do this well, Moni, accepting helplessness. I'm sorry; feeling like this *does* make me bitchy."

"I don't know that I'd be any different in your place. How can anyone know how they would react in your place until they face something like this themselves?"

"It's not going to get me, Moni. They can give me all the prognoses they want, it doesn't mean that I have to believe them. I'll burn this damn thing," she said slamming her hands down on the arms of the chair, "before I let it be my life."

"If you're trying to convince *me*, Marissa, it isn't necessary. I can see how far you've come. That *you're* convinced is what is important. All the encouragement in the world wouldn't make a bit of difference unless *you* believe it can be done."

"It can be," she said, wheeling quickly past Moni. "It *will* be."

Evan swished his hips in a poor Swayze imitation on his way to removing the disk from the DVD player. "So, what's it going to be Mar? If we go with *Footloose* you'll have to make better dancers out of my actors. If we go with *Dirty Dancing*, I'll be making better actors out of your dancers."

"That analysis is meant to make my decision easier, so I'll forgive what sounded like an assumption. Any thoughts from the ladies on the couch?"

There, Moni observed, she did it again—Marissa avoided eye contact with Paige—looked at each of them, then totally turned away when she got to Paige. It isn't my imagination; she's been doing it all day. There is something going on and it doesn't feel like a good thing. Doesn't anyone else notice? She looked at Katherine, who was thoroughly involving herself in the conversation.

"Personally," she was saying, "the romantic in me favors *Dirty Dancing*. Purely a non-technical assessment, however." She looked to Moni sitting next to her. "You and Paige are the dancers—what do you think?"

Moni raised her eyebrows. "Oh, so the sexy dancing had nothing to do with your choice?"

"Of course it did," Katherine returned with a wink.

"Uh, huh." Moni grinned. Not a surprise. It had been years, though, since Moni had danced like that, since she had felt the freedom to express herself with that kind of sensuality. It was a strange realization when, early in their relationship, she had found that it was easier to dance publicly than it was to grant Katherine's wishes for her to do it privately. Weird, she thought, when you love someone so much. "Okay, I'm trying not to cop out here. I like the fact that all the dancers in *Flashdance* are women, and I think *Grease* is a lot of fun and *Footloose* has exciting dances, but I like the drama and sensuality of *Dirty Dancing* more." She turned to Paige, lounging comfortably in the corner of the couch. She'd been typically quiet throughout the movie.

Paige raised one eyebrow in response. "Sex sells, and it's always in style. *Dirty Dancing*."

Katherine offered a coy grin. "And that from the dirtiest dancer I've ever seen dance."

"Is that a compliment?" Evan asked.

"Oh, it's a compliment," returned Moni.

"Hmm," he said, with a none-too-subtle assessment of Paige. He returned his focus to Marissa. "Okay, sweetie, what's it going to be?"

"Like the lady said, sex sells."

Chapter 10

Arranging events that were fun and much appreciated by family and friends was something Jack prided himself on. He liked being in charge and he liked knowing that his ideas resulted in a good time. And lately, he liked knowing that he hadn't lost his touch in the dating world. Today's date with Geri, he had to admit, was one of his best efforts.

They shared a picnic table under the food tent on the grounds of the county Celtic festival. Jack attacked a prehistoric-sized turkey leg as if he hadn't eaten in a week, while Geri tried to pull pieces of hers off with her fingers.

"Honey, this is no place where you have to worry about being dainty," he said, wiping remnants from his mustache with a large napkin. "Don't think they had the same table etiquette we got now."

Geri answered with a relieved smile and took a healthy bite of turkey.

"There you go." Jack followed with a laugh. "Now I know you're having a good time."

Geri nodded and swallowed. "I'm having a great time. I'm glad you didn't think I was stupid for not knowing what a Celtic festival was."

"Hell no," he replied. "Don't know as I would've known myself if it wasn't part of my heritage."

"Where's your family from?"

"Spread all over Wales, but mostly Brecon. My great-great grandpop came over with his new wife and settled in New York. Then sometime in the Forties part of the family migrated to Iowa. I know more about that part of the family than I do the rest."

"Do you have a family crest like the ones over there around that tent?"

"Couldn't honestly tell you," he said, resisting another bite of turkey. "All the investigating I do on the job, you'd think I would've investigated that, wouldn't you? Never did, though, just relied on the tales of Grandpop. Guess I didn't need to know."

"I think it would make me feel kinda special if I knew my family has a crest or a flag or something."

"Yeah," he said, "I s'pose it would." He held up the remains of his turkey leg. "Hey, let's eat up and get over to the other side of the grounds so we don't miss the border collies."

He'd thought of everything, even a blanket and a stadium cushion for Geri to sit on. She was comfortable and having a good time and he was pleased with himself.

Jack pointed to an opening in the crowd of people sitting along the end of the field. "Here come the sheep, a whole herd."

Just as he spoke, the sheep raced into the open field following the lead sheep in front. In a matter of seconds the entire herd was in sight and the sheep began to slow their pace and scatter across the unfamiliar territory.

He pointed straight across from where they were sitting. "Watch over there," he told her.

Geri watched as he had directed and a little black-and-white dog appeared, and with a low, fluid stride began to circle the herd. The collie kept a consistent distance between herself and the perimeter sheep, jutting in slightly to move wayward ones back within her invisible corral.

The little dog continued while her master explained over a microphone how she was working, and Jack watched a fascinated Geri.

Jack had seen the demonstration on two other occasions and

48

each time he was captivated by the intelligence of the little dogs and how tirelessly they worked. One border collie is capable, if needed, of controlling an entire herd—alert to every signal of its master and every movement of the sheep, and resting only when relieved. Even more remarkable is how they can work together, coordinating their efforts and responsibilities in an efficient use of energy and space with no personal agendas or egotism to impede the operation.

If only a police department could work so perfectly, thought Jack. And the court system. Think how much could be accomplished with the same single-mindedness and the dedication of the border collie. But society is no herd of sheep, and even with its limitations he knew the North Branch police force was as good, if not better, than most. And he counted himself as one of the reasons why.

At times like this he even likened himself to the little dog that could. He wasn't a big man by most physical standards, but he watched what he ate and held to a strict daily routine that kept him in better shape than many twenty years his junior. It was a rare morning, even after he made detective, that he didn't complete his regimen of a hundred jumping-jacks, a hundred push-ups, and three hundred sit-ups. He was physically fit and, although he may not have the stamina of the border collie, he had its work ethic. He had focus and determination, and he worked until he was relieved—even further, with a compulsive need to see a case through to its conclusion. He would work off the clock, take his work home or wherever it took him, and solve a case that would've otherwise gone cold and forgotten. Pride in a job well-done. What does a man have if not his pride?

The demonstration was nearly over; the dog master was explaining that working breeds like border collies make good pets only if they are given the space and time for long physical workouts every day. Even at play they must have focus and goal—it is in their nature. Something Jack Beaman understood clearly.

"I just never realized how smart dogs can be," Geri admitted as the sheep were herded toward the trailer.

"Yeah, they're pretty amazing," Jack replied. "I had a little beagle when I was a boy. I swear that little dog kept me out of trouble more times than I could count. Always seemed to know when it was close to curfew and pulled on my pant leg until I started home."

"I never had any pets growing up. Cost too much to feed, at least my dad thought so. I remember telling him once that if I could have a puppy I'd give it half of what was on my plate. He said 'no' and that was the end of it."

Jack rubbed his hand across the top of Geri's back and squeezed her shoulder. "I'm a real believer in kids having pets. They get comfort and joy from them, and they learn responsibility for something that depends on them."

"Another thing I deprived my kids of." Geri looked him directly in the eyes. "Why couldn't I have been a good mother? Their needs weren't any different than mine, why couldn't I see that?"

Jack shook his head and squeezed her shoulder again. "Don't go beatin' yourself up now. I don't believe there are any perfect parents."

"I wonder if Jimmy's new family got him a dog?"

"Have you ever tried to find him?"

Geri dropped her gaze and nodded. "They wouldn't let me know where he is. Afraid I'd interfere with his chance at a new life."

"How old was he?"

"Just turned five," she replied with a distant look in her eyes. "I went to the store to get a cake mix to make him a birthday cake and don't remember anything until I woke up in some motel room three days later. Jimmy had gotten hungry and gone to a neighbor's apartment, and that's when Protective Services came in."

"Ever think about trying to find him now? He'd be old enough to decide on his own if he wants to meet you."

"Almost feels like I should just leave well enough alone—unless he looks for me. He was so young. I imagine him happy and successful, looking for the right woman—a smart woman."

"How about the baby?"

"I don't know," she said, looking at Jack again. "It would be nice to have a name in my mind. Just a first name would be okay. I never even held him, and he had no name. In my heart he felt like a Buddy, like he would have been my little Buddy Boy."

"Was that his father's name?"

Geri shook her head, but offered nothing else.

"What about Annie?"

"Yeah," she said with a nod. "She's the one I need to see again. She's the one I hurt the most. I need to know that she's okay."

"Has she ever tried to contact you?"

"That's the one thing that I taught her well, not to trust me with anything. She learned that early. Don't trust Mom with making sure you have what you need for school, or having dinner ready, or paying the bills, or showing up for teacher conferences. Don't even trust her with your feelings. She'll disappoint you every time." Geri drew her knees closer to her chest and wrapped her arms tightly around them. "So, why," she continued, "would she ever trust me with information that could put her in jail?"

The right answer. No, the perfect answer, Jack admitted. Now how could she give me the perfect answer unless it was the truth? Or have I misjudged the mother as badly as I did the daughter? Is she complicit? Are they capable together of pulling off the perfect crime? He studied her momentarily—chin resting on her knees, the innocence of her posture, the sadness in her face—and wondered if he could really be duped that much.

"I think I knew the exact time she stopped trusting, not just me, but everyone and everything."

Jack let her continue without interruption.

Geri was still hugging her knees and staring out across the field. "It was when she was eleven. I couldn't have told you where I was on Christmas Day, or who Annie's teachers were. I couldn't have even told you who the President was, but I knew the horror in my baby's eyes that day, and what it meant." Geri raised her head and turned toward Jack. "I heard the sirens. Didn't pay them no mind, not until the police were at my door. I don't remember riding there with them, but I'll never forget the sight of her. Little Annie—sitting there in the road with a

51

death-grip on her best friend's hand. Paige was already dead, but the paramedics couldn't get Annie to let go of her hand. I think it's the most horrible feeling I ever had, the most horrible sight I'd ever seen. She was terrified and I knew I couldn't help her."

"What happened?"

"They were on their bikes, just up over the top of the hill there on Rawlings Road. A guy in a pick-up truck, they're always going way too fast on those roads, came up over the hill and hit Paige. They said she died on impact." There were tears in Geri's eyes. "I can't imagine what my baby saw, what she felt."

Jack reached his arm around her and pulled her into his shoulder.

"She knew," Geri said, leaning her weight against him, "that I couldn't help her. And then *I* knew it, too, and after that there weren't no more excuses for me."

He reached into his back pocket and retrieved a folded cotton handkerchief and gently blotted her eyes. His voice had a softness meant for comforting a child. "Here now," he said, "it's long past. You're a different person now."

She nodded against him. "I pray to God that I am."

Jack picked up her hand and held it so that the sun charm on her bracelet dangled in sight. "Did this guy smile at you this morning?"

She lifted her head, but didn't smile. "Every morning," she replied.

"Well, all right then," he said with a squeeze. Then he lifted the tone of his voice. "Hey, we're missing the athletic contests, caber toss, hammer throw, splittin' logs." He offered a hand up and pulled up the blanket to shake it. "There's supposed to be a woman contestant, some been sayin' she can beat most guys."

"That'll be worth seein'," she said.

Chapter 11

Marissa stood beside the walker and faced the mirror that covered the wall of her studio room for the first time since the accident. The scars from the lacerations and the surgeries on her legs were covered by her sweats, giving no visible excuse for her limitations.

She couldn't remember a time in her life, from as early as age six, when watching herself in a mirror was a difficult thing to do. Even when she was awkward in trying to learn the moves, or lost her balance, or had even fallen. It was always the movement, or the rhythm, or the timing that was being scrutinized. Failure just meant doing it again, and again, looking for it to be right—noting the improvement, expecting it to be right, to be perfect. And, eventually, it was.

But this, she looked into her own eyes, this assessment is different. This one isn't about the movement or the timing, this one's about me, about what Marissa Langford is made of—facing where I am and how far I can go. It's time I know. But where do I start?

She stood there, fixed in a stare, while the soundtrack from *Dirty Dancing* changed from one song to the next. Then she closed her eyes, felt an imbalance, and gripped the walker more firmly with her left hand. She began to hum the slow rhythmic notes of "Cry to Me" and let her shoulders keep the beat.

It was the music that had always grounded her, that gave base to her feet and purpose to their beat. And it was the music that let her soar, gave her reason to reach and practice and perfect. It was all she had ever needed—the music and the opportunity to dance. That she had been fortunate enough to make a career out of it was a plus. But losing either one now is unacceptable. Outside Marissa the dancer and Ms. Langford the teacher there is no Marissa Langford.

She opened her eyes once more and concentrated her focus on the movement of her shoulders. The rhythm was there, it was right—the motions understated, reminiscent of a budding dancer afraid of her own talent, but the rhythm was right. She loosened the movements, gave them greater range. Her free arm swept forward and out to the side, her head swayed from side to side, then lay back as she imagined a turn toward an imaginary partner. She could see the movements; feel exactly where they should be. Here's the body sweep, right on cue, fluid and free. She let the move ripple her body in a wave that began in her knees and ended with her head. She was able to ignore the burning from her legs, but could not ignore the loss of balance that nearly sent her to the floor. Her right foot stepped forward hard, catching the weight of her body and sending stabs of burning pain shooting upward to her spine. With an awkward turn she grasped the walker with both hands.

For the next few moments Marissa held herself hunched over the edge of the walker, her body sweating profusely while she struggled to get past the pain-induced nausea. She lifted her head and concentrated on taking deep breaths and letting them out slowly while the words of the song added their assault: "Don't you feel like crying?" Okay, okay. Too soon. She felt a bead of perspiration run the length of her face from her temple to her jaw. Too soon. That's all. No need to panic. It'll be fine.

She straightened her posture as the nausea began to subside. Why today? What made me think I had to do this today? She questioned herself as she ventured another look at the battered body in the mirror. But she knew why. It was no mystery even to her. She had interpreted the look in their eyes the other day.

54

Their eyes all said the same thing; there was less than belief in her ability to come back enough to carry a dance production. They may have tried to disguise it in their words, but their eyes showed clearly what they really thought.

And Paige, well, she didn't even bother to try to disguise it. What a treat *she* was. Being judged by people who genuinely care about me is one thing, but I won't be judged by someone like her—uneducated, undisciplined—an adult version of a street kid. So smug and undeserving of friends like Katherine and Moni. What is it with them? Do they think that they can rescue her? A waste of energy, and of valuable time. At least I had the sense to figure that out in a hurry. What the hell ever possessed me?

Marissa carefully moved the walker into position around her and began to make her way across the room to the doorway and her wheelchair. The discomfort she felt wasn't enough to distract her thoughts. The memory returned again, adding its own complexity of discomfort.

A week-long visit from Paige, probably not much different from this one, and an introduction Marissa could have done without.

"Come on," Moni had urged, "a night out with the girls. We all need it now and again. It's a week night, you won't run into students. And this one," she pointed to Paige, "can really dance."

And dance she could—raw and undisciplined and undeniably sensual. It was clear from the first moment she saw her move that Paige felt the music, that she understood the power of it. With movements that were modish and exciting, she gave the music visibility, interpreting it, having fun with it. It made Marissa want to experience what it felt like to have no bounds, to feel no constraints, no limits, no need for perfection. And to add to the mystique of the night, there was a definite appeal about Paige's confidence, a confidence short of swagger and coupled with a sensual contradiction. It took most of the night before Marissa could identify that what made Paige so unique was a body that butches would line up to bed and the seductiveness of a butch on the make. A woman in jeans and a T-shirt with the moves of a show-girl. The combination was absolutely intriguing.

At first it was fun—letting go like a college student after final exams, feeling young and sexy and carefree. There were stories and laughter, there was the excitement of physical attraction, and nothing at that time in her life that made it wrong to enjoy it. And so she did.

She enjoyed the attention, the looks that singled her out from all the others and made her feel desirable and special. She enjoyed the intimacy of dance after dance, and the touch of Paige's body, and the heat and the tension building from the rhythm of the music. Her mind was free, her inhibitions down. And alcohol, she had to admit these years later, was no excuse for what happened.

What happened was not the result of too much alcohol, it was the result of Paige's hands, confident and sure, finding their way down my sides and over my hips, teasing me from behind, spreading their warmth down the top and up the inside of my thighs. It was the result of Paige's breasts pressing into my back and her hips grinding a rhythm that ignited the most primal part of me. It was Paige's breath, hot against my neck, and the resulting heat that caused desire to pool and the need for relief that sent me into that bathroom after her.

There had been no need for words or explanation; they both knew why they were there. The bathroom cleared, the stall door stood ajar, and within seconds Marissa made the decision to slide, for the first time in her life, into anonymous intimacy.

With her back against the cool metal of the stall, she closed her eyes and her mind to everything except what Paige was making her feel. And it was plenty—as intense a sexual encounter as she had ever had. The *most* intense, if she allowed herself a moment of impartial honesty. Her body shook and her heart raced at opening-night speed. This was a performance she had little control over. Paige pressed up against her and buried her lips at the base of her neck.

There would have been no question as to what was happening in that stall had others entered the bathroom, but Marissa had no conscious concern about that. Her thoughts were stunted into frantic searches for Paige's lips, and gasps and grinds and presses that twisted the tension so tightly that she thought her body would explode before either of them could get her zipper down. What they felt, what they did, was primal and raw. An uninhibited act of sexual release that had started with a single beat on the dance floor and ended with Marissa biting into Paige's shoulder to muffle the sounds of her coming. One leg wrapped around Paige's hips, she pushed down onto Paige's hand. Harder and harder, taking the fingers as deep as she could, while her body exploded in orgasm. And still she pushed, sending muffled shouts into Paige's shoulder as Paige's words seared against her neck, "Yes, baby, yes. I'll give you all you want."

Marissa answered her with a long unruffled moan, tilting her head back against the wall and tightening her grip on Paige's body. She dug her fingers hard into the back of Paige's neck as another spasm, nearly as strong as the first, racked her body. She clung to Paige longer than she wanted, partly to ride out the ripples of sensations that felt so good, and partly because she had no idea how to gracefully remove herself from the situation.

Moments later, however, Paige made it easy. Her voice was soft and free of bravado. "As much as I enjoyed giving you pleasure, no one will know except those *you* tell." She eased gently from their embrace and added, "I'll leave first and bring some drinks back to the table."

So simple, so discreet. Like she had done it a hundred times. Ultimately, exactly the thought that kept returning, and the thought that bothered Marissa most. Just one of many, nothing special at all, just part of the routine. But to Paige's credit, it hadn't been for bragging purposes. To this day, it seemed that no one else knew about it, not even Moni and Katherine. The fact that Marissa Langford had gotten busy in a bathroom stall with a virtual stranger had indeed been no one else's business.

So, if it hadn't been for bragging rights, and there had been no returned pleasure or hope for a relationship, what was Paige's motivation? A purely personal need to please? A private confidence builder? Was it conquests like this that gave her the smugness to carry on a conversation only when she felt like it, and leave without explanation or goodbyes? A rudeness that was forgiven or overlooked by many the moment the serious blue eyes were upon them or she took their hand to dance.

Yet, she does evoke anger in me, even now. And I don't know why. It was my choice to do what I did, and I wasn't looking for a relationship with her. Not really. Giving her my number just invited a call, it didn't promise a date. Does the anger come from the fact that she didn't even try, that I wasn't appealing enough, desirable enough, for even *her* to want a relationship? A selfish and arrogant thing to want just so that I could turn her down. I *would* have turned her down, wouldn't I?

Still unmoved from the doorway, Marissa stared out across the room from her wheelchair. As she focused on the sad-looking figure in the mirror an unnerving thought occurred to her. The days when her own physical appeal was enough to attract even a one-night stand were gone now. Had it been the right choice to spend all those years focusing on a career—performing, teaching, pushing for perfection, all the training and sacrificing? Was it worth not ever having a lasting relationship?

Achievement had been paramount, the kind of achievement that took more than talent, the kind that the women who had wandered in and out of her life had not understood. She had been accused of being selfish and self-centered, and even boring. And to a certain extent, it was true. It wasn't hard to see how dating had become inconsequential and relationships rare and short-lived. Not that she had ever seriously thought that she would be alone for the rest of her life. Somewhere in the back of her mind was the assumption that someday the right woman would come into her life, accept her for who she was, and love her and stay. But it had never been a conscious concern—not until this moment—when the fear of being less than whole, less than capable, less than desirable was suddenly real.

I never saw them as a sacrifice, those years of discipline, the ones that left my mark and validated my life. But they were. Who's going to want me now, with a body full of scars that even I can't look at? Who's going to love what can all too easily become a defeated, useless woman? Only someone who would pity me, a woman whose life mission is to care for the helpless and less fortunate. She'd smother me in sympathy and expect only gratitude in return. And I'd hate her for it because I would hate myself.

"No," she said aloud, "not an option. I'd rather be dead!"

She wheeled her chair abruptly around toward the door. "I *will* get out of this damn chair. I'll teach and I'll dance, and it will be as if this never happened.

Chapter 12

"So, why do you think Paige decided to get a job and stay for a while?" Katherine asked. She handed Moni a linen shirt to hang up to dry and tossed the rest of the laundry into the dryer.

Moni shook her head. "It's so out of character, as nervous as she was last week. I've been thinking about it all day."

"And?"

"It's probably a combination of things. She feels comfortable around us. We know her and accept her for who she is. Maybe she needs some time around people where she doesn't have to lie or pretend."

"Have you ever . . ." Katherine hesitated. "I hope this won't sound . . ."

Moni met her eyes before Katherine could finish. "It will. I'm surprised that it's taken you so long to ask it."

"You're so sure that you know what I was going to say?"

"It's only natural to wonder, especially for someone who doesn't know *her* well."

"You're hedging, Moni The word isn't *wonder*, it's doubt." Katherine leaned against the front of the dryer and folded her arms. "Have you ever doubted her story about what happened?"

"I am hedging—*have* hedged. I never wanted to doubt her. I knew how badly she needed someone to believe her, to believe *in* her. I equated it as one and the same, probably because I needed believing in so badly myself."

"So, do you think that it's possible that it was Paige who killed her stepfather?"

"I don't like that you're making me say this, Katherine."

"To me, and to yourself, not to Paige. It's possible that she is going to be here for a while. We should address the issue, at least in our own minds, as thoroughly as possible."

"She's renting a room in Ann Arbor," Moni said, turning to leave the laundry room. "It's not like you'll have to deal with her on a daily basis. I'm not asking you to harbor a fugitive."

Katherine caught up with her at the bottom of the basement stairs and took Moni's arm. "I understand that, Moni. I appreciate that she is considerate enough not to put us in that position. Really, that's not the issue at all."

Moni's words now had a sharp edge. "Then what is the issue?"

Katherine let her grip loosen and drop to Moni's hand. She looked directly into the defensive blue eyes. "I know that you want there to be a way of helping her. I've explored different possibilities myself. But before you can consider whether we can help her, Moni, you have to be able to separate yourself emotionally. You have to be able to step back and see Paige without seeing or feeling your own needs or your own history."

"My own history is exactly why I understand her. Lack of validation, whether it's from family or from peers, still causes the same struggle for *self*-validation. Aloneness, whether it's self-imposed or otherwise, causes the same amplification of fear." Her defensiveness softened into a frown. "It doesn't matter if she killed him or not. Can't you see that?"

"But it *does* matter." Katherine's eyes were still direct. "It's the only way we'll know whether she needs exoneration, or if she needs defense." Katherine took both of Moni's hands in her own. "The only place that it doesn't matter is in our hearts. That's what I'm trying to say. Step outside your heart, Moni and let's take a good evaluative look at the possibilities. Okay?" she said with a squeeze of her hands.

Moni dropped her eyes from Katherine's gaze. It wasn't possible to dig your heels in and square your shoulders in a stubborn stand while looking into those eyes. At least for Moni it wasn't, even when she was right. But this time she was wrong.

So defensive, Moni thought, always throwing my back up tight to the wall when it comes to Paige. Was it because no one else ever had stood their ground for her, or was it the fear that no one ever would? No one except me. At least that's what I've always thought. Moni looked at Katherine's hands holding hers so securely, then lifted her eyes to Katherine's, waiting patiently for her trust. How many years does it take for trust to grow into its own, to be strong enough to override the fear that your back is open, unprotected?

Finally, softly, Moni asked, "You have my back, haven't you?"

Katherine stepped up level with Moni and wrapped her arms around her. "I do indeed," she said quietly against her head. "Just as you have Paige's, just as we both have Paige's. That's not where the doubt lies."

Moni dropped the basket of folded clothes onto the bed, her thoughts still her own. She spoke them aloud when Katherine's arms closed around her. "She's not going to let us help her," she said, leaning back into the embrace.

"Are you so sure? So sure that you aren't even willing to try?"

"We're in a damn awful position, Katherine. We can't do anything without her cooperation, and the one thing I'm sure of is that she is convinced that any legal investigation will result in her going to prison."

Katherine released her hold and sat on the edge of the bed to face Moni. "Which goes to my thought that she fears that there is no adequate defense for her killing him. And at one time it was a justified fear. There certainly wasn't much of a track record for a successful battered-woman defense sixteen years ago, let alone any defense for a teenager tired of watching, or even enduring, the abuse."

"What if she really is protecting her mother?"

Katherine frowned. "A mother who, for whatever combination

of excuses, never protected her, never even provided for her basic needs? My God, Moni, she fed her like you would a wild animal. Is it logical that she would sacrifice whatever happiness was possible in her adult life for a mother like that?"

Logical? Of course it wasn't logical. Did it have to be? Isn't the lack of unpredictability, that freedom to be illogical, one of the things that set humans apart from the machines they create? Why else would we need shrinks to try to sort through tangled emotions and irrational behavior? Cause and effect isn't always what it seems it should be. Besides, there is so much we don't know about Paige.

"Maybe you're right," Moni finally offered. "I don't have enough information to really know one way or the other. But then, neither do you."

"Granted," Katherine replied. "And if you want me to be a part of this with you, you're going to have to tell me whatever you *do* know."

Katherine waited again while Moni went through whatever thought process was needed, but this time she couldn't resist asking, "Is this a habit that you picked up from Paige?"

Moni's brows pushed into a silent question, and Katherine obliged. "The long silences. I'm never privy to the process that gets you your response."

"But you do get a response. Paige isn't always that accommodating." She returned Katherine's gentle smile. "See, that's part of my history that helps me understand her. We both knew the importance of weighing our responses. I learned early that questions from my peers couldn't be counted on to come from the same innocent motives as those from my family. A question like 'What do you think of the new girl in history class?' was actually bait for an answer they could use to ridicule me. If I said that she seemed nice, they would shout warnings to her that I was going to try to get into her pants. But if I said something evasive like 'she's okay,' then they'd tell her that even the class queer wasn't interested. It became a self-protection to think out the consequences before I answered, or to decide if I should answer at all."

Katherine took Moni's hand and directed her to sit next to her, and let her continue without interruption.

"I wanted friends and I didn't want to be rude to someone who was actually trying to be nice to me, but I never knew who to trust. I wasn't confident enough to fight back, or just to be me, so I withdrew further and stayed to myself. When I found the ball team and Paige I found everything I had been missing at school. They liked me; they accepted me for who I was. And I knew I could trust them."

"That made it easy for you to identify what might be behind Paige's reactions." Katherine noted Moni's nod, and asked, "Did she tell you much about what her childhood was like?"

"Bits and pieces. Mostly I deduced things from comments and how she reacted to different situations. I watched how she acted around her landlady, old Mavis, and around our coach. That distant air, that almost arrogant sense of self-reliance dissolved into a childlike dependence. Although the two were very different, Paige seemed to revere them both with a maternal respect. She listened to their opinions, sought their attention and sympathy at times when she didn't feel well or when she had gotten hurt. I noticed that she protected her private times with them, and it took a long time before she would allow me to share any of that time with them."

"Looking for the nurturing that she never got from her mother."

"It was so obvious, partly because of how it contrasted with the kids in school going headlong into the rebellion-against-their-parents stage." Moni smiled, her eyes locked in a distant stare. "She would cock her head and use this little-girl voice and plead her case, whatever it was, until she had Mavis or Lou Ann hugging her and breaking up with laughter."

Katherine, too, was smiling.

"It's easy to judge someone like Paige if all you've seen is the hard-built exterior—a woman who drinks too much, a person you can't count on to be there when you need her, someone with no apparent concern for the feelings of others."

"A judgment that even you made once."

Moni nodded. "Out of hurt. Maybe that's why I'm so stubborn about defending her now."

"Don't you think it's time that Paige defended herself?"

"Any suggestions on how to convince *her* that she should?"

Katherine traced the outline of Moni's cheek with her index finger. "Other than you being the right woman for the job? No."

Chapter 13

She wasn't Mavis, this stout little woman with her high soft voice and tight white curls. But when she closed her thick fingers over Paige's hand and lifted up a pale hazel welcome, Paige felt immediately comfortable. It was as if she had known Miss Emily for months.

An inquiry about the room for rent turned into sharing tea and freshly baked biscuits and a walk through Emily's garden. They strolled paths the width of a lawnmower that divided sections of perennial beds in various stages of bloom. Bright yellows and lacy whites, busy climbers and names that Paige wouldn't remember tomorrow. What she did take away from their walk was a sereneness, a strong sense of well-being, and the knowledge that this garden, tended by this eighty-six-year-old woman, was in perpetual bloom from April until late October—oh yes, and Emily's favorite song, "I Come To The Garden Alone." It was all she needed to know.

"Miss Emily, would you consider letting me rent the room by the week? I'm not sure how long I'll be here."

"Of course you can, dear."

"I'll pay you ahead for the next week."

Her voice was as light and sweet as the expression on her face. "I don't worry much about that. I know people think that I ought to," she said, taking Paige's hand, "even some from my church.

But the Lord watches out for me." She patted the top of Paige's hand and turned on the grassy path toward the house. "He always sends me someone special."

Put *that* way, Paige doubted that there would be many who would want to hurt this woman. Even if someone stiffed her for the rent or stole every cent she had in the house, Miss Emily would most likely figure they needed it and leave it to God to take care of their conscience. Actually, Paige thought, Emily had it wrong—*she* was the special one. And it was fate, not God, providing one of its rare opportunities to enjoy the feeling of comfort she knew Emily offered her.

It was no mystery why she had turned around on the highway to spend time with Moni and Katherine. In a life of so few constants there is a recognizable need to see familiar faces, to share time that's free of the unknown, time that allows conversation to begin where history left off. It was a comfort that Paige rarely experienced. It was a time to rest.

Many people don't realize, Paige had decided, how much comfort comes from family, from knowing someone and being known by someone your whole life. Or the luxury of having a life-long friend, someone who shares the knowledge of exactly who the other person is, with all their faults and accomplishments and growth. To accept and be accepted, without possibility of pretense, was a privilege most people take for granted—a privilege rarely possible in Paige's life.

Emily's voice broke into Paige's thoughts. "Here's your key," she said. "I like to keep it on this ring. A little neighbor girl made this little piece at camp for me." She smiled proudly and handed it to Paige. "You can park right here at the end of the driveway and use this door. You won't disturb me a bit, even if you come in late. Come on now, I'll show you where the laundry is."

The thought suddenly occurred that staying here might be too easy. It had been unexpectedly easy once before, with Mavis—wonderful old Mavis, caring for that part of Paige that she knew and unfazed by what she didn't. She listened when it was needed, emanated an aura of wisdom and surrounded Paige with a sense of well-being that she had never known as a child. Before she knew it, Paige was solving crossword puzzles with Mavis on week-nights, watching favorite TV programs with her and sharing breakfast every morning. It felt like what she had imagined a real home would feel like, and it had been too easy to stay there for well over a year. The sense of well-being had overridden her instincts. She played softball for a full season. She made friends. She was happy. And when well-being became entitlement, she slept with Moni—too young and too innocent for what that meant. After that, she knew that it wasn't *if* but how much she would hurt Moni. Reality flashed itself in neon that next morning, and Paige heeded its warning quickly. She would have to leave sooner or later, and sooner was sure to be the less painful. She would not do to Moni what she had taken months to do to Audrey Graves. It was selfish to love, and to be loved, in vain. And she would not stay here long enough to take the chance of that happening with anyone else.

Chapter 14

Sunday morning had begun early. Ever since his birthday, Bradley wouldn't sleep past six-thirty. He wanted to play with his new fire truck every minute that he was allowed. It was his favorite thing in the world right now and Jackie didn't have the heart to say no.

On weekdays it didn't present a problem—it actually made it easier to have him ready to drop off at Rachael's. But weekends, and especially Sundays, Danny stayed over and slept in.

Jackie dressed her thirty pounds of wiggle in the bathroom where his excitement wouldn't wake Danny. "Shhh, okay, okay, now remember, no siren until Danny wakes up."

Bradley raced to the living room, dropped to his knees next to his prized truck and made sure that all the ladders and lights worked just fine. He ran the truck on a path on the hardwood floor outside the area rug and maneuvered it around the perimeter of the room, going under the end tables and behind the couch.

With a smile, Jackie turned her attention to last night's dishes and a fresh pot of coffee. Today was going to be a good day. She'd have everything ready for a nice breakfast as soon as Danny got up and then they would spend the day together like a family. Bradley could sleep on the drive to the zoo—they'd take him to see his ever-talked-about pandas, and it would be a wonderful day.

It hadn't been easy, dating, finding a man to share her life with, when her first priority was her child. It was amazing how fast a grown man could disappear at the first sight of an infant. A ready-made family is a sure romance killer. But Danny hadn't run. His patience wasn't what hers was, but he tried. He worked hard, took a job at Meijer's that he thought was below him, and drank only socially. And when he said that he loved her, she believed him.

The apartment was quiet, with only the occasional sound of a car coming or going in the adjacent parking lot. Jackie finished the *'O' Magazine* that she hadn't had time to read all week and poured herself a fresh cup of coffee. She stopped in the doorway at a sight that negated all the challenges of single parenthood. Bradley had fallen asleep on the floor, his little butt in the air and his arm over his fire truck.

"My sweet little guy," she whispered, and knew that if she had it to do over, she'd make the same choice all over again.

Minutes later the bedroom door opened and Danny muttered something sleepily before disappearing into the bathroom. Canadian bacon and eggs over easy were on his plate when he emerged freshly showered.

"Thanks, I'm starved," he said with a kiss to her cheek. "Did you already eat?"

"I ate when I fed Bradley. He was up so early."

"Make him stay in bed on the weekends," he said, diving into his breakfast, "so you can sleep in."

"I don't mind. It gives me a little time to myself while he's playing."

Bradley appeared momentarily in the doorway, then scampered back into the other room. The fire truck siren accompanied his imitation of a running engine.

Jackie smiled. "He was so good about not making noise while you were sleeping."

"Yeah, he's a good kid," Danny replied.

She poured him another cup of coffee. "Do you want me to fix you more eggs?" When he shook his head, she added, "We'll probably end up getting a late lunch. He'll want to see his pandas as soon as we get there."

"We'll have to go another weekend," he said matter-of-factly.

Jackie turned quickly from the counter. "Why?"

"I've got some things I need to get done today."

She dropped into her chair and met his eyes. "Can't they wait? He's been looking forward to this all week."

"He'll forget about it until we bring it up again."

"No, he won't, Danny. You haven't heard him all week. He's so excited about seeing the pandas." She watched him drink his coffee and waited for a response. When he rose from the table without one, she continued.

"Let's not disappoint him, okay? I'll help you do whatever you need to get done when we get home."

He picked up his plate and put it in the sink. "We'll go next weekend," he said over his shoulder.

She faced him as he turned. "You promised him, Dan."

"Well, plans change." He left the kitchen and started through the front room.

Jackie followed. "Wait, Dan. Why won't you discuss this with me?"

He stopped and turned. "Look. I've just got things to do, okay?"

Bradley pulled at the pant leg of Dan's jeans. "Look, Danny, look," he said raising the ladder of the fire truck.

"Yeah, Brad," he replied without looking.

"What do you have to do? Is it that important that you have to change plans at the last minute, or is it that you just don't want to go?"

Bradley tugged at his pant leg again. "Look, Danny." He hit the siren on the truck.

"Stop it, Brad," Dan said, pulling his pant leg from Bradley's grasp.

"Let's not discuss this in front of him," Jackie suggested. "Come back to the kitchen with me."

"We're not going, Jackie. That's the end of it."

"Dan, I think I deserve an explanation. It's one thing to disappoint me, I'm an adult, I can understand if there's a good reason—but he's three."

Dan's normally good-natured expression had been replaced

with a sharpness that she had seen only once before. That time it had been pushed in the face of an umpire who had called him out on a close play at the plate.

He raised his voice. "And *I'm* an adult, and the last time I looked there was no ring on my finger that says I have to pass every decision past you."

"Don't yell in front of him."

"I'll yell," he said even louder, "if I want."

Bradley scooted backward toward the couch and tried to pull his truck with him. When he grabbed it the siren went off again.

Turning toward Bradley, Dan yelled, "Stop it!" And before Jackie could stop him, he stomped down hard on the truck, breaking it into pieces.

Bradley jumped and blinked, then his face contorted around a deafening wail.

Dan shouted again, "Stop it!"

Jackie rushed to pull Bradley up into her arms. "You stop it!" she shouted back. She cradled Bradley's sobs into her shoulder. "What's wrong with you?"

"With me?" he said, grabbing Jackie's arm. "What's wrong with *me*? What the hell's wrong with you? You can't just let something be."

"Let go of me," she demanded. "You're hurting me."

He squeezed harder, and pulled her a hard step toward him. His words were hissed through clenched teeth. "Don't you tell me what to do."

Jackie lowered her voice. "You're hurting my arm, Dan, and you're scaring Bradley."

"Oh, God," he spat with sarcasm, "we don't want that now, do we?" He tightened his vice-like grip to its last notch, held it while he stared into her eyes, then released it with a hard push.

Jackie caught her balance. "Why don't you go now," she said in a soft voice. "Get your things done. I have to calm him down."

Dan brushed by her to the bedroom, grabbed his wallet and keys, and said calmly as he left, "Why couldn't you have just said that in the beginning?"

Chapter 15

Marissa dropped heavily onto the seat of her wheelchair as Dr. Bingham rolled his stool around to face her. Maybe the dread she felt toward this visit wouldn't have been this great two months from now, or three. Just a little more time and she would have shown him, she would have walked the distance he required, pushed the strength meter to the proof he needed. But, maybe . . . she looked into his eyes and fought a pang of fear; maybe he could see how much she needed this.

"Well," he said with a professional smile that failed in its mission, "you are one of the most amazing patients I've had the pleasure of treating." He placed his clipboard of notes on his lap and clasped his hands together on top of it. "You have progressed further than I ever would have guessed." He hesitated, searching her eyes, choosing his words carefully. "I know how much you want to return to teaching, Marissa. But I think you know what I'm going to say."

She pulled her eyes abruptly from his and stared hard toward the door of the examining room. A walking Marissa would have been through that door already. Yet her instinct to flee was stalled by her own hands frozen at the top of her chair wheels.

"I wish I could tell you differently," he continued, "but there's been no significant improvement since your last two exams. You're at a plateau, Marissa, maybe permanently."

"I need to work harder, that's all," she said firmly. "If you could just sign the university form and tell them I need a little more time. You know I'll work hard."

"I can't tell them what I don't believe to be true. I'm afraid that how hard you work doesn't have anything to do with the result we're seeing. Dr. Clark concurs with me; it may not get any better than this." He reached for her hand, but she pulled it away. "I'm sorry, Marissa."

Marissa wheeled determinedly down the hallway and into the lobby where her sister was waiting. Dr. Bingham followed solemnly behind her.

Christina rose to greet her and quickly assessed the situation. "Marissa—"

"Take me home, please," Marissa said as she wheeled by her.

This time there was no attempt at even a professional smile from the doctor. "This is a tough day for her," he said. "Maybe the toughest one so far."

"She's not going to be able to teach, is she?"

"Not in the way the university expects. I don't want to discourage her from working for more improvement—God knows I was wrong about her prognosis in the beginning—but I won't lie to her either."

"No one expects you to, Doctor. It's one miracle that she is alive, and another that she is self-sufficient and able to live on her own." There was deep concern in Christina's expression. "If she weren't this capable I'm afraid she'd try to end it."

"That's why I can't emphasize enough how important it is for her to see a therapist."

"I know," she replied. "And I've encouraged her to see someone, even gotten recommendations for her, but she's—"

"Stubborn," he finished. "Which I'm not going to fault her for because that's partly why she has gotten this far. What's important now, though, is for everyone to realize what a drastic change this means for her life, most likely a permanent change. She's going to need all the patience and understanding we can give her."

"It's hard to know what to say to her. She doesn't complain.

She just gets angry if you don't have the same expectations of her that she has for herself. But how do you tell her that they are too high?"

The doctor shook his head. "Get her to see a therapist. Christina."

"I'm her only sister," she said, looking to the end of the hall where Marissa sat waiting. "But even when we were children I was never able to talk her into anything she didn't want to do." She turned back to the doctor. "That doesn't mean that I'll stop trying, though."

Marissa stared straight ahead during the drive home. Uncharacteristically, she answered Christina briefly and only when necessary. She wheeled herself up the temporary ramp that her brother-in-law had insisted on making, and Christina invited herself in.

"I'll be fine, Chris," she said without turning around. "Thank you."

"I wish you would talk to me, Mari. It's not good to keep it all inside."

Marissa wheeled to the opposite end of the living room and stopped in front of the large window that overlooked the small backyard. She stared silently, leaving Christina to decide whether to pursue a conversation or to leave her sister alone.

A moment later, Christina was standing behind the chair massaging Marissa's shoulders. "What did you say the name of this one is?" she asked, manipulating the large muscle extending from Marissa's neck.

"Trapezius."

"Does it still cramp a lot?"

"Not much anymore."

They both let silence fill the chasm between them, Christina unable and Marissa unwilling to find the words, until Christina made another attempt.

"I guess I've never known how to talk to you. Maybe we're just too different. As much as I've always loved you, and admired you, I've never known how to let you know that."

"I do know, Chris . . . I know."

"Then how do I help you?"

After another few seconds of silence, Marissa replied, "There's nothing you can do, nothing anyone can do."

Christina let her hands rest on Marissa's shoulders. "Remember when Uncle Aaron broke his neck diving into that lake, clearing it out for the scouts? We were so little then, and all we wanted was for him to live. Remember how we prayed?" She waited for a response but didn't receive even a nod. "And how hard he worked? How excited everyone was when he could move his fingers? He always had that tennis ball in his hand, squeezing, all the time he was talking to us. I don't think there was a craft he didn't learn to do. You wouldn't sit still long enough, but when I was old enough he taught me how to hook a rug. Remember that beautiful rug Mom had in the den? His rugs won prizes all over the country, and that one won more than any of them, so he gave it to Mom."

Marissa continued to stare silently out the window. She hadn't wanted to think about Aaron; in fact, she had consciously blocked the thoughts of him from her mind many times since the accident. He, too, had proven his initial prognosis wrong—progressing from a quadriplegic to gaining the use of his upper body and at least partial use of his legs. But the best he could do, with all the years of work and therapy, was to walk short distances with crutches braced to his arms. And as much fun as they had thought it was as children to ride on his chair as he maneuvered it in fancy turns and wheelies, she couldn't allow the thought that she would spend the rest of her life in a chair.

"Teaching physically challenged kids," Christina continued, "wasn't what he had planned—physical education and coaching were no longer possible—but he became Teacher of the Year three times. And look how instrumental he has been lobbying for the rights of the handicapped. Our very own uncle testifying before Congress all those times. He's been a hero in so many lives."

Marissa's voice was soft, despondent. "I'm not going to be anyone's hero, Chris."

"I doubt Uncle Aaron foresaw that he would be, either. He just took what he had and did the very best he could with it, and look what happened!"

But he already had his life-mate and three babies, counting on him and loving him. And he had something else—a will, an unshakeable drive that kept him fighting impossible odds. His drive let him find another place where his best was enough—not just for others, but for himself. "Before today, I would have said that I had a drive equal to that challenge. But now . . ."

"Now you've got *my* girls praying for you like we did for him. They're a lot older than we were; they understand better how much you've accomplished already. You *are* a hero to them, Mari, and to me, and I'll bet to a lot of your friends. You've only started—you're going to do wonderful things," she said, stroking Marissa's head, "just in a new direction."

"I'm going to need some time alone, Chris." She turned her chair and offered a weak smile. "Time to think about that new direction."

Christina nodded. "Okay," she said, returning the smile. "I'll call you tomorrow."

"Thank you, Chris, for everything. I love you."

Chapter 16

The answering machine blinked as it had every day all week when Jackie returned home from work. She knew what the message would say, but she hit the button anyway. Bradley dragged his bag into the front room as Dan's voice pleaded his case once again.

"Honey, I'm running out of ways to apologize. I don't know what more I can say. I love you and I'm sorry. You're the best thing in my life, baby. Give me another chance to show you how much I love you and make it up to Bradley. Call my cell, baby. Please?"

She hit the erase button. She would ignore this one just as she had the others, and the flowers that went immediately into the trash can at work, and the notes left on her car. There were moments when she was sure that the right thing to do was to file a restraining order. And other moments when she was just as sure that she could forgive him and start afresh.

But it wasn't only herself she had to think about. She crossed the living room where Bradley had crawled onto the couch and fallen asleep. He missed his truck. He missed Danny. How could something so simple on one hand be so complex on the other? We all get angry, we all lose it now and then. Isn't forgiveness the bigger part of the equation? At least as far as Bradley was concerned, it needed to be.

Quietly Jackie closed the apartment door behind her. She opened the trunk of her car and removed the box she had intended on returning to K-Mart tomorrow. Her own confusion wasn't going to keep Bradley from having his truck, no matter if Dan did pay for it.

Jack Beaman hadn't taken two steps inside the door when he was almost knocked off balance by a pint-sized Bradley with no brakes.

"Careful, honey," Jackie said with a smile. "You're going to knock your Popu over."

"It's okay," Jack replied. "You're just glad to see Popu, aren't ya?"

Bradley gripped Jack's leg tightly and nodded against it.

"And how's my girl?" he asked, accepting a kiss to his cheek. "Have you had a good week?"

She offered a half-hearted smile, but was saved from an explanation when Bradley grabbed Jack's hand and pulled him toward the couch.

"Popu, look," he said and scrambled behind the couch. He backed out, butt first, pulling his fire truck into view. "My new truck," he said with excitement.

Jack chuckled. "I'd say he likes that truck all right if it's still *new* after a month."

"Yeah," Jackie returned. "It's his favorite thing." She knelt beside Bradley. "Hey, honey, can I talk to Popu for a little bit while you play with your truck? Then, I'll bet he'll let you take it with you to his house tonight. Okay?"

"Okay," he said with a nod.

In the kitchen, Jackie placed a glass of his favorite beer in front of her father and settled into the chair across from him.

"It's been a long time since you've *requested* consul with your ole' man. Is everything okay?"

"Did you and Mom argue before you were married?"

Jack smiled. "Enough for me to know what I was getting into. No shrinking violet, your momma. She let me know right away that pants were meant for one purpose only—to cover hairy, white legs. What she did or did not wear on *her* legs had no bearing on her place in this world."

"So, it was kind of an identifying process? Making sure the other knew who you were."

"I'd be kinda suspect of marrying someone I never argued with. Surprises have a funny way of laying a path to divorce court."

Jackie sipped a soda and looked closely at her father's face. The lines were deeper now—creased from laughter, furrowed from stress. A good face. One she had always been able to read and to trust. She had counted on him more than she realized. Always there with a comforting hug. No wonder Mom loved him.

"What did you argue about?" he asked.

"Spending Sunday taking Bradley to the zoo. He backed out at the last minute and expected me to make it all right with a three-year-old."

"Have you both had time since to think about it?"

"All week."

"What've you got figured out?"

"Not sure what he's got figured out, guess I'll find that out tonight. For me, I see that he isn't as ready for the family thing as I thought he was . . . I know he loves Bradley. They've got this special handshake greeting thing, and he spends time one on one with him without me having to ask him to. It's not easy to find a man who doesn't bolt the minute he knows you have a child. But maybe I've been assuming too much."

Jack patted his daughter's arm. "It takes longer for guys. You know—the minivan replacing the pick-up truck, it's harder for guys to make that change."

She smiled at his candor. "Yeah."

"You love this guy?"

"Faults and all," she replied. "And I let him into my son's life and now Bradley loves him, too. He's been moping around all week. I can't let my own anger get in the way of what's best

80

for him. Maybe I just need to give Dan more time and not push him."

"You work it out however you can, honey, and as long as he is an honest man, works hard, and is good to you and Brad, then he'll never have to answer to your ol' man. Otherwise, he'll be payin' the devil for a free ticket."

Chapter 17

The music announced the bar's existence up to a block away. It bounced at louder than safe decibels off the walls and ceiling and reverberated through the floor. Bodies, predominantly male, waited and leaned, squeezed by and suggested, and danced with abandon as Paige maneuvered her way to a vacant spot along the wall. She placed her drink on the ledge and looked to the dance floor. Lights flashed over a mass of flailing arms and grinding hips, illuminating faces she would have no need to remember tomorrow.

This was her comfort zone. Until Derrick had gotten sick she had spent more hours in gay bars than she had in their apartment. Derrick. It was hard not to believe that he would be appearing any minute, drinks held above his head, smiling his way through the crowd toward her. "Oh, honey," he'd say, his eyes gleaming mischievously, "I need a cigarette after that trip." It made her smile even now, right past the tears that were trying to blur her memory.

It was time that she did this—face the loss on familiar ground. Packing up her few belongings and walking away from the apartment was too easy really. She never had to sort through his things, his other friends did that. Never had anything but memories to haunt her. She had simply walked away, disconnected her life from anything still connected to his, and moved on. But the loss, she soon realized, was everywhere she went. Maybe now she could face it.

She realized, a moment later, the familiar dark blue eyes staring at her from a few feet away were not Derrick's. Evan Adams approached with a welcoming smile that gleamed white in the darkness.

"Paige, isn't it?" he asked, nearly shouting and extending his hand. "Evan. You met me at Marissa's a couple of months ago."

"Yes," she replied in the middle of a warm handshake.

He moved in closer to avoid shouting. "You looked as though you were trying to place me."

"No, I remember you."

"Are you here alone?"

Paige nodded.

"Come on," he said, taking her hand.

They made their way back through the crowded bar to the other side, further from the dancing mob to an area of small tables. Evan motioned to an empty chair next to one draped with a leather jacket.

It had been many years since Derrick had taken her by the hand and led her across a bar. She'd been so young then—they both were—and everything had been so exciting. They were on their own, watching out for each other, and ready to find the good things in life. They were sure that they had left the worst behind them.

"This is as close to conversation level as it gets in here," Evan was saying.

"Are you here alone, too?" Paige asked.

"Not really. I know a lot of people here." He offered her a cigarette and she refused. "I usually meet a couple of friends and hang out for a while on Friday nights, but they didn't show tonight. What's your excuse?"

"Don't have one."

He stared at her for a moment as she turned her attention to her drink. Finally he asked, "That's it?"

"That's what?"

"The only explanation you're going to give me."

She looked him directly in the eyes. If only they were Derrick's eyes, with their promise of faithfulness and honesty. "I came here to drink a little, dance a little. Cheap therapy."

There was the beginning of a smile, followed by a frown. "But a guy's bar?"

"Keeps me out of trouble," she replied.

This time the smile found its full range. A nice smile, Paige thought, glistening with little-boy honesty.

"I'm between boyfriends," he offered. "Looking for trouble."

Paige finally returned the smile. "This looks like the place to find it."

Evan took a quick drag from his cigarette and nodded. "I'm not really looking hard. This is just a good place to get away from the day-to-day nasties. For a few hours I let loud music and laughter crowd out all the things that bother me. I don't know if it does anything to make things better—they're still there the next day. But I go at them with a better attitude."

"Nothing wrong with that."

His attention wandered about the bar, smoke curling from the neglected cigarette between his fingers. Paige leaned back in her chair and sipped her drink until his attention returned. "I talked with Katherine last week. She checked in on Marissa while I was there . . . She actually suggested that I talk with you."

"*Me*?"

"I hesitated even asking if Moni had any time, I know she's really busy." He brought his eyes directly to hers. "Marissa's in bad shape."

"Moni mentioned that she had plateaued or something."

Evan shook his head. "No, it's much worse than she or Katherine know."

"It's more than physical?"

"Not being able to teach has knocked her right on her ass. I saw it coming, but . . . you were right. I remember what you said that day."

"Yeah, reality's not going to cut you any kind of break. You're better off if you look it right in the eye."

Evan stubbed out the cigarette butt in the ashtray and released an exasperated sigh. "Well, she's not even in the fight any more—she's not following through with the lawsuit, not returning phone calls, not doing her therapy. The rest of the staff and I are carrying the production plans forward right now, but we're going to need someone to fill her responsibilities pretty soon . . . It's her chance to show the university some progress . . ."

"But she's not progressing."

"I was hoping that Moni would have some time to help us out, since Marissa's impressed enough with her dance skills to have her working with her in summer theater," he explained, "I hoped she could sort of buy Marissa some time to get back on track. But there's no way she can fit in that many hours . . . There's so much I just know Marissa can do, if only she believed it."

"*Can* she get back on track?"

Evan pressed his lips tightly together and flexed the large muscle in his jaw.

Paige drew her own conclusion. "So, you think I could help buy her some time, just in case."

"You'd be paid. The money's been budgeted for it."

Paige didn't allow even a second of consideration. "I don't have any training for it."

"That's why I—we—thought if you worked with Marissa, you know, just to get some direction, then you'd be helping us out and maybe her, too. She'd have something to be responsible for."

"What about her responsibility to the show and to you?"

He shook his head. "It's too overwhelming for her . . . Hey, just give it some thought, okay?" He pulled a card from his jacket pocket and wrote on the back. "Here, this is my home number. Take a few days, really think it over. Otherwise, I have to ask another teacher and Marissa will most likely lose one more piece of her career."

Paige took the card and held it for a moment before pushing it into her jeans pocket. "I hope Marissa knows how lucky she is to have a friend like you."

"We've been friends for a long time. I know the heart of her—the real her. There are things I've entrusted to her, sensitive

85

personal stuff I wouldn't trust my family with, shit I wouldn't even trust a lover with, and I've never regretted it."

He was beginning to speak a language now that Paige understood. She began to listen to what was behind his words.

He continued, leaning forward now, his arms on the table. "Marissa is the kind of person who understands sacrifice because she's lived it—it's not cognitive with her, it's life. She really understands what it is for a student to work their way through college, to have no financial help, because she did it herself. And she knows the price of it, for college, and beyond if they want to perform. There's a big part of life, socially and personally, that you give up because you dedicate everything toward becoming good enough, and then to staying good enough."

"Where did she perform?"

"Off-Broadway, Canada; she toured with a dance company, choreographed many of the original performances and danced Martha Graham's masterpiece works. It's tough. So much talent vying for so few opportunities. And the age consideration is for real; you only have a few years to make it happen."

"Then you teach," Paige concluded.

"If you're lucky and if you're good with people. Teaching's not a given either. It takes a lot of patience. You have to believe in what you're doing. Marissa does." Evan raised his eyebrows. "I don't think she could tell you how many extra hours she spends with students. And the money. There've been times, I don't know for sure how many, that she's spent her own money to make tuition for students who were in danger of dropping out." He held Paige's gaze as he spoke. "Can you see why, friend-wise, I feel like I'm the lucky one?"

"Yeah," she replied. "I see."

Chapter 18

Two days later, Paige was standing outside Marissa's door while Evan rang the bell and pounded.

"She's not going to answer," he said. He fished the keys from his jeans pocket. "I had to let myself in last time, too."

Hesitantly, Paige followed him in. "I don't like this, Evan. She doesn't know I'd be coming with you."

"That's what happens when you don't answer your phone and you let your voice mail fill up."

He strode to the middle of the living room and called. "Marissa? Mar, it's Evan. Where are you?" When there was no answer, he peeked into an empty, spotless kitchen, then turned quickly toward the bedroom.

"What?" Paige asked.

"It doesn't look like it's been touched since her sister cleaned it last week." He knocked at the partially open door and called more softly this time. "Mar, it's Evan. Are you all right?"

The reply from the bedroom could barely be heard. "Go home, Evan. I'll call you tomorrow."

"Sweetie," he said, peering around the door, "that's what you said last time. You know how I hate waiting for phone calls, even from you."

He motioned for Paige to stay where she was, and entered the room.

Paige could hear the tone of Evan's voice but not much of what he was saying. It was soothing and reassuring, so much like Derrick's in the middle of the night when fears had gotten the best of her. She envied Marissa having Evan in her life. It had been such a long time since the sound of Derrick's voice had promised her safe-keeping. She had never once questioned whether he really had the ability to protect her, even after adolescence had morphed into adulthood. Nor did he ever question her ability, even at the end when the strength of her hand was all he knew. It was Paige who questioned then, when hopes and prayers and medicines had all failed, it was she who could no longer believe in anything.

She could make out some of the words now, clearly Marissa's voice. "I don't want her here," then Evan's calm tone, and Marissa again, "I don't want her help."

There was more undecipherable conversation, and some moving about in the room while Paige weighed whether or not staying was the best choice. She had just decided to leave, when Evan emerged from the bedroom.

He held up his hand to halt her retreat and motioned for her to follow him to the living room. "Look," he said quietly, "I really need some support here. Her sister's been out of town. She won't be back for another week."

"Hey, I don't know that I could be of any help even if she wanted me to."

"It doesn't matter what she wants, you didn't see what I just saw in there." The concern that pressed his brows together was enough to keep Paige listening. "I don't think she's eaten since her sister was here; I don't think she's been out of that room. I forced her out of bed and into the wheelchair and told her that we weren't leaving until she got showered and came out here to talk to us."

Paige offered her own knitted brow. "I guess I can at least give you moral support." She took his direction and joined him on the couch.

His face showed relief, but his words did not. "This is not the Marissa I know. I never expected this. Everyone was so thankful that she made it out of that mess alive, and hopeful when her recovery went so well. We didn't realize the impact this whole thing would have on her life."

Paige listened, watching this man search for a way to help his friend, knowing in her heart that she could not really help him. She could at least offer him moral support, let him know he wasn't alone, encourage him. But she hadn't been able to help Derrick and she could barely help herself, so to pretend that she could do anything for Marissa would be ludicrous.

Before she could figure out how to diplomatically tell him, though, a loud thud sounded from the bedroom. Evan bolted from the couch and Paige followed him into the bedroom.

The air was foul, a mix of odors consistent with neglect. The shades were drawn, the room in disarray, and Marissa was sitting on the floor next to the bed.

Evan bent over and offered his hands. "What happened, Mar? Are you all right?"

She replied without taking his hands. "Just leave, Evan. Let me be."

He persisted. "When did you eat last?"

"Get her out of here, Evan, please."

"I'll go," Paige offered quickly.

Evan turned to face Paige, his expression reflecting his concern. "I'm sure that we're both in for some verbal abuse here, but I'm asking you to stay and help me." He closed the distance between them and took Paige's hand. His voice was low. "She's very shaky," he said. "She's in real trouble."

Paige consented. "I'll follow your lead."

Evan squeezed her hand and turned back to Marissa. "We're staying here to help you, Mar, because we care about you." He knelt in front of her and continued, "You have a lot of people who care about you, it's you now who has to start caring."

"If you really cared," she replied, "you'd respect my privacy."

He moved to Marissa's side and motioned for Paige to take the other. "Come on," he said, "let's get you back in the chair."

They took hold under her arms, but Marissa struggled against their grip. "Let go of me. I can take care of myself."

"But you aren't," Evan returned. "And I'm not going to stand by and watch."

This time they muscled her up and into the wheelchair despite her protest. "You were headed back to bed, weren't you?" Evan asked. When Marissa didn't answer, he leaned forward and placed both hands on the arms of the chair. "I don't want to be disrespectful, but the choice I'm going to give you may make that impossible." He held Marissa's hard stare without flinching. "You can either go in there on your own and shower, or Paige and I are going to put you in there."

She spoke in a harsh whisper directly into his face. "I don't know who you are anymore."

He straightened, ignored her insult and wheeled her into the bathroom. "Okay," he said, "what's it going to be?"

"Get out of here and shut the door."

"As soon as I get clean clothes for you, I'll do just that."

The water ran the whole time that Paige and Evan changed the bed sheets, straightened and cleaned the room, and opened the window and freshened the air.

Evan approached the bathroom door just as the water stopped. "Good," he said, raising his hands. "I was starting to worry."

Paige placed the now empty waste basket back in its place. "So, when we leave, what's going to stop her from continuing on this destructive course until it gets even worse?"

"God, I wish Christina was here."

"Even if she was, Evan, Marissa didn't get to this state overnight. If Christina hasn't been able to change the course, what makes you think we can help at all?"

"Nothing," he said, dropping heavily to sit on the bed. "I'm grasping, Paige. You can see that, can't you? Shit, I'm asking a stranger for help."

"I'm not exactly a stranger, but I know what you're saying."

"I don't know what I'm saying, or what I'm expecting—even of myself. I'm no miracle worker. Friends and family can only do so much. We can't force her to want to try, and that's what makes me angry."

"Then how angry must she be?"

Evan stared momentarily into Paige's eyes as if the last letter of a crossword puzzle had fallen into place. He clenched his jaw and lowered his eyes with a nod.

"Do you still want me to try to help with the show?"

"Yes," he quickly answered. "That much I do know."

"What if she's not willing to show me what I need? I'd be useless. You'd be better off asking another teacher to help."

"Even if you only get us through the auditions, up to when I absolutely have to have professional help. Think of it as a part-time job to give you a little extra cash. This show is an important part of the department's financial structure." He looked toward the bathroom door and added, "She's put in so many years; I'm not ready to give up on her yet."

Paige gave him a slight smile. Grasping? That's nothing to be ashamed of. Doing this for the extra cash would be shameful. Is that what I'm doing this for? Can I claim any better motive? An answer—yes or no—is all he wants. I don't have to know why, not yet anyway. "I'm only working part-time hours at the store. I can be wherever you need me after one o'clock."

"My first class is at eleven. I'll do my best to see that she's up and dressed by the time you get here."

"And if she doesn't let me in?"

"I'll show you where the emergency key is."

"Evan, I'm not comfortable invading her privacy like that."

"How comfortable are you with what we saw today?" She didn't answer him, but it wasn't necessary. "It's part of what I'm paying you for—you can't have a lesson if you can't get into the classroom."

"What if there are no lessons?"

"We'll cross that bridge when we get to it."

The bathroom door opened and Marissa wheeled slowly through the doorway. She made no eye contact, and said only, "Please leave now."

Evan turned to Paige. "Go ahead," he said. "I'm going to chance further abuse and fix her something to eat."

"I'll call you later."

Chapter 19

Jack sat in his usual booth, hands wrapped around an untouched cup of coffee. His staring at the comings and goings in the parking lot was interrupted as Geri placed a fresh cup in front of him and sat down.

"Must be something serious bothering your mind," she said.

"That's the problem," he replied. "Can't decide if it's serious or not."

"If it's got you bothered . . ."

"Yep," he said with a nod. "It does." After a sip from his coffee he continued. "I don't like what's coming together in my head. It's one of those times when you want to be wrong, but you're afraid you're not."

Geri waited as he organized his thoughts.

"I was trying to pinpoint what first started my thinking on it. It was the fire truck—Bradley's fire truck. He kept calling it his new truck, but I had gotten it for him a month before. And then, while I was talking on the phone, he hit the siren. When I told him to keep it quiet for a few minutes he started crying. I finally got him to tell me that Dan didn't like the siren and had broken his truck. So it really was a new truck."

"Kids should be allowed to be kids—they shouldn't suffer when it's the adults that have the problem. I know that first hand."

"Well, that was the start. Now I'm puttin' other things together in a pattern after that. Like the screen on Jackie's front window all pushed in and her telling me that she locked herself out and she knows I've got the extra key with me right here in my wallet." His brow formed a scowl. "And just yesterday I saw a huge bruise on her leg, and I wouldn't have thought so much about it, but she tried so hard to keep me from seeing it. If she tripped over Bradley's toys and fell like she said, why would she care if I saw it or not?"

Geri broke eye contact and scanned her empty section of the restaurant.

"See, I wanna hope it's the cop in me scrutinizing things that aren't there."

Her eyes came back to his, then dropped quickly to his coffee cup. "I'll get you a fresh cup. You're doing more talking than sipping."

Jack reached out and took her hand as she rose. "Wait, I'd like to know what you think. I don't want to be Jackie's paranoid ol' man, you know?"

"Have you met her boyfriend?" she asked, easing back into the booth.

"I have," he nodded. "That's why I'm thinking so hard on this. Good strong handshake, looks me square in the eye, treats me with respect. A Cubs fan, but I can't hold that against the guy."

"What does Jackie say?"

"Nothing that don't sound natural to the mating ritual. She says she really loves him, got real about the white-knight thing some time ago. She's a smart girl, Geri. I can't believe she'd let any guy . . ." He stopped and looked hard into her eyes. "Tell me I'm just being a paranoid ol' man; I'd rather be that, I'd much rather be that."

He kept his eyes on hers until she was compelled to answer him. "It ain't always about being smart. There's other things that cloud up how you see everything. Times when they're treatin' you good, they get to shinin' up brighter than the other times and you remind yourself that nobody's perfect." She shifted in her seat and leaned forward over her folded arms. "Sometimes you stay because you love them, sometimes it's fear that makes you stay."

"Well now, that's where I've got some major understanding problems. A woman with normal faculties is gonna figure out that love ain't gonna change a man like that, and I can't believe that she'd keep trying if he's physically hurting her. And fear, well, that's even easier—you just get the hell outta there and get help."

Geri looked as though she would say something, but instead pressed the back of her fingers against her lips.

"What is it?" Jack asked.

"Nothin'. I should see if they need me in the back."

Jack persisted. "What did I say?"

Then a look of resolve as Geri spoke. "I stayed out of fear."

He stared back, unsure of where, or if, the conversation should go from here. Her eyes dropped from his stare. He hadn't meant to insult her. Finally he asked, "Do you mean Randall?"

"RJ. He hated 'Randall.'"

"What were you afraid of?"

"Of stayin', but more of leavin'."

"Did he hit you, or was he threatening you?"

"He was mean when he drank," she replied, meeting his eyes once again. "It got so that it didn't matter that the bruises showed."

"But there were no reports, nothing on file. Why didn't you get help?"

"I called once. After they left he nearly beat me to death. I'd embarrassed him in front of the guys he worked with. I never called again."

"See now that's why the law says we have to prosecute if we see signs of abuse because women refuse to press charges."

"I saw how they talked with him that night, joking and smiling like they were coming from a ball game. When I came to I was lying on the floor in the narrow space between the bed and the wall where Annie had dragged me. It don't take a genius to figure if an eight-year-old is your protection that the signs won't ever matter. He was one of them." She rose from the booth and added, "You're one of them."

He was looking at her back, unable to respond quickly enough before she disappeared around the counter and into the kitchen.

"Yeah," he muttered to himself. "Of course I am." What did that *mean*, that she thinks *I'd* look the other way? Or that I'd abuse her too? And now what—I'm suppose to go after her? And say what?

Jack rested his forehead in the palm of his hand. I'm no damn psychologist. I don't even know if I believe her. No reports, no real efforts to get help, and no indications that a respected member of the force had crossed the line. *Was* there talk in the department? I don't remember any. Hell, lots of guys drink after work. Could Officer Buschell have had a problem and no one knew about it? Why the hell would she lie about something like that? Damn, I don't know *what* I know anymore.

He sat there for a long time, trying to remember anything to substantiate Geri's claims. He remembered listening to RJ tell the others his stories of working on the SWAT team in Iowa City, and how exciting it had sounded to be in on the action and the big busts. His partner, who had trusted his life to him every day, was devastated at his death. Hell, the whole department was. They hadn't lost an officer in action in twenty years, and then to lose one that way. It hadn't been easy for them to move this one to the cold-case file. All the more reason for Jack Beaman to not let go of it.

He had convinced himself to go talk to her, diplomatically of course, when Geri appeared beside the table.

"She's stayin' out of love," she said. "I'm worried about your daughter."

"She's not going to tell me, is she?"

Geri remained standing, her expression unreadable. "What would you do if she did?"

"Somebody'd better give him a head start . . . shit!" he spat. "I just answered my own question . . . Can she do this without me?"

"I still ain't got it all figured out—what puts two people together and makes a prison with bars you can't see. But I'm trying to learn about it. I don't ever want to be in that prison again. And I can't stand it to see someone else there."

"As long as you're clean and sober, why would you worry about that?"

"What if that's not all there is to it for me?" she asked. "And it wasn't just me—he stayed, too. Why didn't he walk away?"

Jack pondered. Because he thought you'd quit drinking? He loved you? Obviously he didn't realize how dangerous a sixteen-year-old girl could be. Actually, "I don't know, Geri. I only know that I have to decide whether I should confront Jackie again, or get into Danny Boy's face and hope that I can control myself to only scare him into a conscience."

"I have a book I want you to take to Jackie. It's helping me understand things some. Do you think she'd read it?"

"What kind of book?"

"It's by a psychiatrist, but it's easy enough to read. She talks about signs that could mean danger in a relationship and what she thinks makes some guys become violent."

His eyes, serious and pensive, held hers. "You think this is serious, don't you?"

"Would you want to guess wrong?"

Chapter 20

Jack finished reading the last page of the book and closed the cover. He sat in his favorite reading chair, glasses still in place, staring at the title. *Till Death Do Us Part*. The words made him uneasy, anxious. The same feelings that used to stall the pumping adrenaline into stale pools of nausea when he looked into the eyes of a guilty man and knew that he couldn't prove it.

Could this be the same thing? Is the danger that the doctor describes the same danger that Jackie faces? Some of the things fit, but certainly not all of them. Sure, Dan's been in and out of jobs, but so have a lot of guys. It's harder now, not like when companies took care of their people. Loyalty isn't a cherished value anymore. Bouts of depression? Well, yeah, that goes with the job insecurity. So, there are no outward signs of drug abuse or social isolation. How could Dan be the deadly threat that the book talks about?

Jack placed the book on the lamp table next to his chair and rose to retrieve the newspaper from the couch. Jackie's a smart girl; she wouldn't put herself in jeopardy. She certainly would not put Bradley in harm's way. What am I thinking? Is this what professional burn-out is, when your job invades the sanctity of your private life? Am I seeing *everything* through professional, skeptical eyes? He stood in the middle of the room, newspaper in hand. What surer way to lose the trust and respect of your own daughter than to wrongly go nose to nose with the man she loves and threaten to make dog food out of his balls?

He opened the paper and returned to his chair. Besides, what kind of idiot would chance hurting the daughter of a police detective? Not a smart move. Jack settled in again and pulled out the sports section. He skimmed the scores and flipped to the high school games, but nothing was able to hold his attention. He folded it and dropped the paper next to the chair. A minute later he picked up the book and headed out the door.

Jackie's face brightened noticeably as she emerged from the side door of National Bank's Third Street branch. "Daddy," she called. "What a nice surprise."

Jack climbed from the car and hugged his daughter. "Hey, sweetie, did you have a nice day?"

"Not too bad," she returned. "I've only got one more customer account to get signed up to make goal this month."

"If you get stuck you know you can get me into another cd."

"I'll be fine. Did you want to come have dinner with us tonight?"

"No, I've got a bit of patchin' up to do with Geri tonight. Sort of hurt her feelings without meaning to. Can we just have coffee across the street and talk?"

"Sure, Dad." She dug her phone from her purse. "I'll give Rachael a call and let her know I'll be a little late picking Bradley up. I'll take her a piece of her favorite cheesecake and she'll forgive me."

The book lay on the chair next to Jack until a comfortable buffer of small talk softened the edge of his real purpose. He began carefully. "You know your old man might be a stubborn old bastard, but he's also smart enough to admit he's no expert on women." He chuckled at himself and continued. "I hobbled home on one foot, pulled the other out of my mouth, and read this book Geri gave me."

He picked up the book and set it down in the middle of the table.

Jackie spun the book around and began to examine it. "What did you say to her?"

"I was less than supportive regarding women staying in abusive relationships. Then she tells me that her relationship with her husband was abusive, and tried to choke some education past the foot in my mouth. She settled for the book. Now I've got to admit that I'm not so smart after all."

"Was she talking about the husband that was killed?"

"Yeah, he was on the force with me when I had a beat. It surprised me to hear that about him—it got me worrying about you again, sweetie."

"Please just *stop* worrying about me, Dad. I told you everything is fine. We have our arguments like most couples, but there's nothing to worry about. You told me yourself to be suspect if we didn't argue."

"I know, I know," he said with a slight grimace. "But, remember that I'm no shrink. I don't know everything, just what I've seen in my life. I'm sure there are a lot of things I missed seeing—like with Geri's husband." He clasped his hands together and leaned forward on the table. "I want you to be sure that love isn't keeping you from seeing everything clearly."

"He's a good man, Dad. He's trying to get a good paying job so that we can get married. He wants me to be able to stay home with Bradley."

"Do you want to quit working?"

"I like my job well enough, but he's right, I should be home while Bradley's little. I've already missed so much. Rachael got to see his first steps and hear his first words. I don't want to miss any more."

Jack took his time, thinking over his next question, debating whether to ask it or not. It seemed the kind of thing he'd end up kicking himself for no matter which way he went. So, "Jackie, I want you to look me in the eye and tell me that Dan has never physically hurt you, that you'd never let him hurt you or Bradley."

She did look him in the eye, then as she began to speak, her eyes shifted left and back again. "He hasn't hurt me, and you *know* that I would never let anyone hurt Bradley. He's my life, I'd never allow that."

The words were what he wanted to hear; actually they were exactly what he had expected to hear. But were her eyes telling him something else? His training, and a good amount of experience in interrogation, had taught him a few things about truth and the human psyche. Very few people can lie with their eyes square on yours—the pathological liar, that rare individual with absolutely no conscience—but not the rest. And a shift to the left is a clear sign of a lie. But was Jackie's shift that clear? Could she have merely shifted focus toward the movement of the waitress passing by? This is no interrogation room, stark and controlled; it's a busy public place for God's sake. Speculation is out. I know nothing more now than I did before I sat down, and I'm not going to ask her again, at least not today.

"Daddy, I know that your worrying is coming from your heart, but I'm a big girl now. I'm okay. Really."

"Will you do something then, just to humor your old man?" He pushed the book to her side of the table. "Read the book. At least maybe you can help me understand what happened to Geri."

Jack watched her, with her eyes on the book, hesitating. For what? For fear that he will see the book? What would that matter if he wasn't guilty of anything that was in it? And what if he was? The questions stopped when she picked up the book, only to slam it back down on the table.

"You need to let it be." Her voice had the tone of teenage rebellion. Her words stood defensively mature. "This isn't about Geri, it's about me." She stood abruptly from the table. "I'm not your little girl anymore. I'm an adult woman. I don't need you to tell me who to love or how to live my life." She held up her hand as if to prevent him from responding. Her voice softened slightly. "I need you to just be my father. Just love me."

As she turned to leave, Jack rose and gently took her arm. "I do," he replied. "So you need to hear one thing, even though I've said it before. No matter where I am, I'm at the other end of that phone. You call me if you ever need me for anything."

Chapter 21

Paige rang the doorbell of Marissa's house for the third time. Just because Evan told her to use the emergency key if she had to didn't make it any easier to do. It felt way too much like breaking and entering someone's house when you know they are home. She was going to be an unwelcome intruder regardless of how she looked at it. She reached for the bell one more time when she heard the turn of the lock.

The grateful feeling that she didn't have to use the key was quickly extinguished by Marissa's greeting. "Oh, good. The second half of the baby-sitting squad is here." She turned her chair briskly and wheeled away from the door.

Paige followed her without a response.

"Don't bother to check the garbage," Marissa continued, "Evan wouldn't leave until I ate his idea of breakfast."

"I wasn't going to check anything, Marissa. What you do or don't do is your business. I'm here to learn whatever I can to help Evan with the show."

Marissa whirled around to face Paige. "And just what is it that you think you can do to help with my show?"

Her tone was unmistakably indignant and condescending. Paige was tempted to match it, but resisted. "I don't know, Marissa, maybe nothing."

Marissa turned her chair and wheeled down the hall and into the dance room.

Paige followed, stopping abruptly just inside the doorway when Marissa whirled the chair around again to face her.

Marissa gestured with her arm toward the center of the room as she stared coldly at Paige without a word.

"This is a fine room," Paige said. She looked uncomfortably around the room, then reluctantly brought her eyes back to Marissa.

Marissa continued her icy stare until Paige pulled her eyes away, then asked, "So, what *is* it you think you can do to help me?"

"Well, Evan thought—"

"I know what Evan thinks."

Paige matched the icy stare with her own, stoic and unreadable, but it didn't deter Marissa. "Is he paying you?

"Yes, he is."

Marissa nodded as though it was the expected answer. "The opportunist strikes again."

The reference was as obvious as it was inexcusably wrong. And it was all Paige could take. "If you've got something to say to me, you'd better say it now—this'll be your last chance to do it."

Marissa seemed stunned, unable to respond.

"Go ahead," Paige quipped. "Get it out there . . . What? You gonna hold it for another four years? Ten? Forever? Say it."

"Yeah. Okay. I'll say it. I don't like you. I don't like your arrogance, or your presumption that you have anything I need." She spat her words with more energy than she had exhibited in weeks. "You're a street dancer, a bar dancer. You know nothing about sacrifice and discipline, and I doubt you ever will. You ramble through life, no aims, no goals, no commitments, wasting God-given talents like they were cheap giveaway prizes. It makes me sick to my stomach. I can't stand being around you."

Paige waited, eyes unflinching from a cold stare, until she was sure the barrage had ended. She made her wait, gave her no indication that her words had had any effect. When she did speak, her voice was strong and firm, and devoid of emotion. "I don't care what you think of me. To do that I would have to respect you, and I don't. I did once, when I first met you. Not so much what you had accomplished, but the determination it took to get there. But you're not that person anymore."

She wondered why Marissa didn't demand that she leave. She wouldn't leave, she decided, even if Marissa did demand it—not until she had her say. "I know you're angry, it's all you can see in your eyes now. The sparkle and laughter and life are all gone from them. They're ugly now, ugly with anger. And that's the one thing I understand about you, because I've finally been able to understand it in myself. Don't worry, I won't burden you with any of the cheap personal stuff, I rarely dump that even on people who care. But you are going to hear one thing before I leave—maybe it'll matter to you, maybe it won't—but you're damn well gonna hear it."

Paige took a step closer and leaned forward. "That anger that's making you bitter and ugly? It's gonna get you sympathy for only so long—then it's going to kill you. And if that's what you're going to let happen, it would have been better for everyone if you had just died in that accident."

Marissa's eyes narrowed, and her lips parted as if she would respond, but closed again without a word.

"So I'll leave you to do whatever you want to do. You're in no position to teach me anything anyway."

Paige paced the floor of the tiny rented room, waiting until she was sure Evan would be home. What the hell did I do, besides ruining any chance I had of getting any kind of help from Marissa? Arrogant—she hit that one on the head. What else would allow an uneducated bar dancer to think that she could preach to someone like Marissa Langford? I haven't earned that right. I'll never earn that right.

The only thing I've earned, and *earned* is a questionable claim, was one brief chance to give her pleasure—my one chance to thank her for sharing her beauty, for letting me smile with her laughing eyes and feel the movement of her body as the music found its course. She was so exciting to watch, all polished and fine, pushing past the edge of refinement and technique to show me that she understood passion. And I knew that she did, even before she let me be a part of it.

I knew when her eyes danced over my breasts and my hips, before they locked onto my eyes and drove their message home. I knew from the heat of her hand finding its way around my waist and flattening itself against my abdomen, before her hips ground their rhythm against my own. I knew, so I took her passion and seared it hot against my mouth, let her take it deep and hard and long, and turned that passion wet against my thigh until it took me in.

What I didn't know was the depth her passion would take me—hard and fast, ridden to the most primal place. I could feel the depth of it in the tightness of her grasp, digging into my shoulders and entwined in my hair, and the desperation of her cries. And then, erupting like an uncontrollable force of nature, I could feel it in the power of her climax.

I didn't ask about her passion—where it came from, where it might lead. I let her own it, free and clear—hers alone to explore, to share, or to keep secret. I don't know if she knows that. I want her to.

She checked her watch once more, then quickly dialed Evan's number. She continued to pace as she spoke. "Evan, it's Paige."

"Please tell me the tone of your voice is just the result of initial learning frustration."

"I'm not going to get the chance to be frustrated," she replied, "at least not by Marissa. And I take full responsibility for that."

Evan let out a sigh on the other end. "Shit."

"I'm sorry."

"Me, too."

"Look, Evan, I've been thinking about this all afternoon. You've still got to hold auditions, and if she was going to use some of the choreography from the movie for that, I can study the tape and learn it on my own. Maybe I can at least get you past the auditions."

Evan's voice was noticeably more upbeat. "We tape each audition and all the readings so that Mar and I can review them for casting. She'll have a hard time giving up those decisions to anyone else."

"But the show choreography—"

"We won't worry about that yet," Evan insisted. "I'll drop the tape off to you tonight. And Paige, thank you."

"Don't thank me yet."

Chapter 22

The fury that had been pounding in Marissa's head for days without relief finally erupted in a barrage into the phone. "What the *hell* where you thinking, Evan? What gives you the right to try to force that woman into my life? I do not want her involved with the show—that's yours and mine. And I don't want her around me. How could you do this?! You don't know anything about her!"

When she stopped for a much-needed but shaky breath, Evan took his chance to respond. "You haven't been acting like this is your show. What do you expect me to do, get one of your colleagues to take over the last—"

"I expect you to be my friend, Evan. Please," she pleaded, fighting frustration and tears, "not this woman. Okay?"

"Look, honey, I'm not going to get angry and I'm not going to hang up on you. But I'm also not going to argue with you. So, calm down, breathe deeply and slowly, and let's talk about this."

She complied, mainly because without the anger she didn't know what to say. She knew she was spreading a wide net of anger, an unfairly wide net, but she didn't know how to pull it in.

"Okay," he began, "it's pretty clear that there's something going on here. And since I'm getting the brunt end of whatever it is, it would be nice if you'd fill me in."

"I'm frustrated, Evan. I'm tired, I'm in pain, and I'm frustrated."

"That's because you are stubborn to the point of being unreasonable. You refuse to take all your medications, you refuse professional help—"

"My insurance won't pay for any more therapy."

"I mean psychological help. God, Marissa, you may be the only person I know who's never seen a therapist, and probably the one who could benefit the most from it."

"Thanks, Evan, exactly what I'd expect to hear from a friend."

"I didn't mean for it to sound like that. I'm trying to say that sometimes you can't do it all by yourself. It's like not being able to see the forest for trees—you're too close to the problem. It takes someone else to help you see the whole picture. Then you can work on solutions."

"I know what the problem is."

His response carried a sarcastic edge. "Then how is that solution working?"

There was a long pause before Marissa offered her own sarcasm. "Thanks for being such a big part of that solution."

"Look, being bitchy isn't going to make me hang up, and it's not going to make me tell Paige that we don't need her. So, that said, why don't you tell me what your problem is with her."

"It's personal, Evan."

"Jesus, Marissa, so is having Mother Nature surprise your lover at the most inopportune time, but it didn't stop you from sharing *that* with me."

"I don't like her."

"And I'm not particularly fond of Harold Jenkins either, but he's a hell of a set builder, and we'd be in desperate need without him."

"She's an opportunist—taking *what* she can *while* she can."

"Then it should make you feel better knowing that I'm doing the same thing to her."

"Oh, good," she exclaimed. "Maybe you can also become arrogant, and while you're at it, start wasting and abusing your God-given talents."

"There it is."

"What are you talking about?"

"The problem—that one you weren't going to put into words."

Her tone was firm, her words clipped short. "The problem is I don't like her."

"No, the problem is that she can still do what you can't."

The anger that had rendered her speechless earlier made a swift return. Without another word Marissa clicked the phone dead and threw it into the pillow at the other end of the couch.

Best friend. Confidante. Never a traitor. Not Evan. Never would I have expected this of *him*. Haven't I always supported *him*, been there whenever he needed me? Right beside him, beside the conflicted gay man at his mother's funeral, beside the jilted lover who never saw it coming? Are *my* needs any less important? Can't he respect them even if he doesn't understand them? Wouldn't I do the same for him, no questions asked?

But no, he can't do that. *He* has decided what I need, made judgments about what I think and what I feel. Take your meds, see a therapist—everyone's solution for Marissa Langford's successful re-entry into their comfortable world.

Comfortable? For *them*. If they can get their friend, their sister, to at least look as though she's not about to self-destruct then they can relax and stop worrying about her. And that would be wonderful. But they won't be the ones going through the process—the unavoidable, solitary process of grieving over a loss. Only I can do that—it's my loss. It's my career that was cut short, my talent that was taken away, my grief. So I'll go through the stages, for as long as it takes, because I have to—alone. Through the denial, through the anger, and, if I'm lucky, maybe someday into an acceptance of my plight. The course is clear, only the timeline is in question. I don't need a therapist to tell me that.

Chapter 23

For days she had put off this phone call, but it had to be made sooner or later. Marissa made herself comfortable in the afternoon sunlight of the living room window.

Evan was the one friend she could never deny, the one who readily forgave and was always forgiven. He'd stayed away, given her time, waited patiently for the anger to subside. And it had, at least toward him, at least enough to make this call.

She began with, "I just wanted to call to—"

"It's me, Mar, Evan Dean the drama queen. There's no need for an apology. I just want to know that you are all right."

"I'm all right," she said, then added quickly, "I won't work with her, Evan. You do whatever you need to do for the show, I understand that, but just keep her away from me. I can't work with her."

"Mar, I want you to be part of this show. I—we—all need you to be. You're very important to the quality of this production—"

"I don't know what I can do. You don't know how hard it is for me to admit that I can't do what I used to, and that there is nothing I can do to change that."

"You're right, I can't know how that feels. But I do know you. I know what's inside and I know you'll get to it—you'll draw from it—you'll find a way. You just have to have time . . . You hearing me, Mar?"

"Yes."

He continued. "You need to give us time, too. Let us get past the auditions, okay? Then let's see."

"Yeah," she replied, "we'll see."

Paige's words kept coming back to her, for weeks now, like a bad strain of a song that won't leave your head. Marissa moved the walker slowly into her dance room. She knew why they wouldn't leave her alone—they were true. The anger *has* made me ugly, as ugly on the inside as the scars are on the outside. That's what people see—the ugliness.

Why did *she* have to be the one to say them? Why couldn't it have been Evan? He's here every morning making sure I get up, get human, eat, at least once a day. He can say it, he sees it. Or Christina. Aren't sisters *supposed* to tell you the truth when no one else will? How ironic it is that it takes someone who doesn't care about you to tell you what you need to know.

Marissa sat on the bench near the mirrored wall and faced the middle of the room. The polished wood floor, unused for so many months, needed to be dusted. She used to love this room. It was the reason she bought this house. Now she hated coming in here. Hated seeing herself in the mirror, hated having to face never being able to use it again.

What do I do now? The anger is more than I can bear. Paige is right; it is going to kill me. I'm letting it kill me. Marissa gripped the edge of the bench tightly, her head dropped back as the tears began. It had taken this long for them to come, this long to give in to them. And now that they had started there was going to be no stopping them. They streamed down the side of her face and into her ears. Marissa hung her head and cried. She cried for a long time, harder than she ever had before as an adult.

When the tears finally did stop, she made her way through the darkened house to the couch and fell asleep.

With the answering machine still turned off, the phone next to the couch rang through the end of a deep sleep. Once she was awake enough to realize that the ringing wasn't part of a dream, Marissa cleared her throat and answered it.

Evan's voice had that tone she had dubbed "boring shit done" and it brought a smile to Marissa's face.

"So I thought I'd bring the audition tapes over," he said. "Is now a good time?"

She cleared a froggy throat again and replied, "What time is it?"

"Noon," he said. "Saturday. And your ass better be out of bed."

"Oh, it is." She glanced down at the sweats still on from yesterday. "And dressed."

"Good," he said and chuckled. "I'm outside. I'll let myself in."

Marissa quickly straightened her clothes and smoothed back her hair. She stood up and reached for the walker as the front door opened.

"Tapes," he announced, sliding a blue milk crate down the hall, "and lunch."

Lunch was the traditional decadence of a cheese-lover's, fully loaded pizza that they rewarded themselves with at this junction. Marissa met him at the kitchen table. "I haven't earned that."

"I have," he said, opening the box and sampling the contents with his fingers. "And you will."

"You're so sure," she said to the smile barely containing the first mouthful of pizza.

There was something very appealing about the smell of familiar, delicious, and admittedly bad-for-you comfort food. It had already skipped right past the reasoning center of her brain and went directly to the appetite center that had been suppressed for many months.

She fetched two sodas from the refrigerator and matched Evan bite for bite until they had thoroughly stuffed themselves.

"Okay, Isadora," he grinned, "time to pay up."

He made everything seem so normal. It was Marissa and Evan as it had been for the past six years, at least for this afternoon.

Marissa rearranged the pillows behind her back. "Is Stan working on the music arrangement?"

Evan nodded and changed tapes in the machine. "He'll have something for us to listen to this week." He dropped back down on the couch and smiled. "Wait until you see this one," he said with a click of the remote.

The young man on the tape was good. He had learned the choreography and performed it flawlessly. But what set him apart from the others was a confidence and personal flair usually found in more mature dancers.

"Where did *he* come from?"

"Transferred in from somewhere," Evan replied. "He's obviously had some formal training."

"Obviously. How was his reading?"

"Not as pretty as what we just saw, but we've got no one else who even comes close to having his combined abilities."

"And you still like Vanessa for the female lead?"

"Yeah, I saw no surprises in those auditions."

Marissa separated a stack of tapes from the others on the coffee table. "Then we have our leads."

"Now the fun begins. You up for a couple more hours of this today?"

"Whatever you want," she replied. "Tomorrow, too."

As Evan leaned forward, she reached over and ran her fingertips over first one scapula and then the other. "What will you do with them when they're too big to hide under your T-shirts?"

He was clearly puzzled.

"The wings you're growing," she said and smiled.

"Oh, that's one that even my mother wouldn't believe." He placed his hands on his waist and twisted his torso forward and back to flash imaginary wings. "Archangel Evan."

Her laugh was the light, easy expression that had all but disappeared since the accident.

He flashed her his most charming smile. "Whatever it takes to get my friend back."

"I may not be worthy of that kind of devotion, and all I can promise you is that I'll try to be worthy of it."

"You don't have to promise me anything," Evan replied.

"But I do, because I haven't been able to promise myself anything."

He nodded his head in acceptance. "Like I said, whatever it takes."

"I had decided last night before I fell asleep that I would call you today and, if it wasn't too late, I wanted to offer you whatever I'm capable of, for both the show and for our friendship. But you beat me to it."

"Patience isn't my strong suit," he said, pushing another tape into the machine. "Ready for some more decisions?"

Marissa hesitated while he returned to the couch. When he met her eyes she said, "Paige did a good job with the auditions, didn't she?"

"She did a great job."

"I figured we had set a pretty big blaze a burning on that bridge."

Evan smiled. "Really? She didn't say."

"Yeah. I set one at my end and she set one at her end. How did you get auditions out of *that* smoke?"

"I haven't a clue," he said with a shake of his head. "Maybe you should ask her."

Chapter 24

The air was crisp and cool, the sky clear of even the thinnest clouds. A perfect fall afternoon. Jack wiped his finger on the wet rag and smoothed the caulk neatly along the edge of the window pane with his index finger.

At the next window, Geri carefully painted the long-neglected trim. "I can't remember the last time this house had fresh paint," she said. "I haven't had a paint brush in my hand since I was a teenager."

Jack wiped his hand clean and went over to check on Geri's progress. "You're doing a mighty fine job, too," he said, wrapping his arms around her waist and kissing the back of her neck.

"Stop that now," she said unconvincingly. "You're going to make me mess up."

"Why don't we take a break," he replied with another kiss to her neck.

When he relaxed his arms from her waist, Geri turned quickly and dabbed his nose with white paint.

"Oh!" he exclaimed. He wiped his nose as she ran for the back-yard.

Seconds later his pursuit took him racing around the corner of the house, side-stepping a lawnmower and, with Geri's retreating figure in sight, cutting across a patch of unmowed, shin-high grass. Right in the middle of the thought to turn and circle back to surprise her, one foot dropped ankle-deep into a depression and sent him sprawling through the weeds and grass face first.

His first instinct was to get up and brush himself off and hope that Geri hadn't seen. But she had seen it and was hurrying back to him, unsuccessfully trying to keep from laughing.

He was up on all fours and she was asking through half laughs, "Are you hurt?"

"I'm not sure which is bruised more, my body or my ego." He sat down and inspected his right ankle. "What'd ya give me on that last dive?"

"Weren't you supposed to point your toes?"

Jack leaned back on his hands and laughed. "At least give me some points for difficulty. That wasn't easy."

Geri sat next to him and brushed dirt and grass from his face and shirt. "We better get ice on that ankle."

"I think my knee took the worst of it," he said rubbing it carefully. "But no matter how much it hurts, I am not gonna go limpin' into work Monday."

Geri leaned over and kissed Jack's cheek. It made him smile.

"You think I'm just an old fool?" he asked.

She stroked the side of his face. "That would make us two old fools."

"For a minute there I was in that blue and gold jersey again heading for the goal line."

Geri smiled. "And I was one of those cheerleaders you guys were always chasing."

He slid his arm around her waist and pulled her into a kiss. A nice kiss, not their first, but not one that would pressure Geri into anything more than she wanted. He'd let her tell him how far she wanted this to go. He had his own dilemma to deal with; he wouldn't add another dimension of guilt to his already conflicted purpose. He'd rather not have to tell a woman he's sleeping with that he was hell-bent on arresting her daughter. Part of him wished she wasn't returning his kiss as genuinely as she was; part of him was thoroughly enjoying it. He hadn't anticipated liking her, not like this.

The plan had been to get to know her, just enough to establish her trust and glean whatever information she had. Chances were she had information she didn't even know she had. And if that were the case, it wouldn't take all that much trust. *That* much trust he was pretty sure of.

Another thing he hadn't figured on was that *what* he had gotten to know about her, he liked. Oh, he hadn't lied to her about wanting to ask her out in high school. He had wanted to. But who she was then wasn't who she had become, and he was surprised to find the person she was now. It went further than respect for turning her life around, as difficult a task as it apparently was to admit addiction, get sober, and stay that way. It was more than sympathy for losing her family and the prime years of her life. It had something to do with an untouched sweetness that drugs and alcohol and maybe even abuse hadn't been able to strip away from her.

Geri had settled into Jack's embrace with her head on his shoulder. Jack placed a kiss on her forehead. That sweetness was what made this situation much more difficult than he had imagined. It left him searching for an acceptable compromise that was realistically impossible. He wanted her to trust him, to like him. Yet, he knew that the minute he got anything he could use to track Ann, even the slightest lead, he would run with it and destroy every good thing she had ever thought about him. It was only a matter of time.

"You think we ought to get back to work?" he asked, stretching his leg out with a groan.

"I think we're getting ice on that knee there, number 34."

Jack laughed and stood slowly. "Better retire that jersey, wouldn't you say?" He hobbled behind her into the house and sat obediently at the kitchen table.

Geri busied herself filling a plastic sandwich bag with ice and wrapping it in a dish towel. She placed it over his knee. "There," she said. "I'll get you a couple of cookies. What do you want to drink?"

"Whatever you got. You don't have to fuss so, Geri."

"I don't mind. I didn't get to do it the first time around." She placed a glass of milk next to his plate and joined him at the table.

"I'd see the cheerleaders bringing cookies and brownies for the guys on the bus, and I'd bake cookies at home and imagine what it would be like to be a cheerleader. Everybody thought they were special and I wanted people to think I was special somehow, too."

"I guess they were special in some ways," he replied. "But they aren't perfect, Geri, none of us are. I always wished I was built bigger so I'd have a chance at the pros. But wishin' it don't make it so."

"I learned that quick enough, when I was young and living with an alcoholic father—all I wanted was to be someone else . . . but there was something I didn't learn until it was too late." She lifted two more cookies from the cookie sheet and placed them on Jack's plate. "When I got sober, I sorted through school reports that I'd thrown in a box and didn't remember ever reading. I found out that Annie told everyone that she and her best friend were sisters and that she was adopted. It was the first time I remembered my heart actually aching. I sat and cried for the longest time. I had driven her away from me way before she actually left. I broke my own heart."

Jack watched her dab tears from her eyes with a napkin and searched for something to say that would make her feel better. He took her hand and squeezed it. "Hey, now, there you go beatin' yourself up again. We get older and wiser and we all figure out we can't live someone else's life. It's just part of growing up." It sounded feeble, but it was the best he could come up with. "I'm proud of you, Geri," he said when her eyes finally met his, "for finding the best of who you are."

Chapter 25

The phone call from Marissa hadn't been a complete surprise. Paige hadn't, however, held her breath in anticipation of it. The improved progress report from Evan was the surprise. She hadn't expected that the harsh barrage she had unleashed on Marissa would have any positive effect. For a couple of days afterward she had struggled with guilt that she may have made things worse, and debated whether she should apologize to her. But there had been no apology from either of them, only a request to continue working on the show and Paige's acceptance to do so.

"This is strictly business," Marissa had informed her. Not that Paige had any delusion that the phone call could mean anything else. "There won't be a personal relationship," she had continued. "I have to do whatever I can do to help Evan; it's a personal and professional obligation to him." Again an explanation that had been unnecessary. "All I ask of you is to do your best to learn the choreography and relay it to the dancers. I don't expect miracles, just an honest, concentrated effort. If you can give us that then I'm willing to work with you."

Marissa hadn't added *for Evan's sake*, but her meaning was clear anyway. And since it was the same reason that she was willing to extend her stay and try working with Marissa, Paige made that commitment.

If it had been Derrick asking her, needing her, there would have been no hesitation to do whatever she could. But Derrick was gone and there had been too few times in her life when she had felt truly needed—when some ability she had could really make a difference to someone else. The feeling it gave her was remarkably good. So, for Evan, she would give her best.

Since then it had been four weeks of choreography, practice, and a carefully controlled working relationship. No personal discussions, no disrespect, and no social time between them. And it worked. Marissa choreographed the show numbers to fit their stage and to showcase the abilities of their dancers. Paige learned and practiced the choreography and taught it to the dancers. Evan, in the meantime, had been able to return his enthusiasm to directing. A scenario that a month ago had been wishful thinking at best.

Paige's voice had a ready-to-burst exuberance to it as she waited for Miss Emily to settle into her favorite chair in the living room.

"I finally got it, Miss Em. It looked like such an easy move," she explained as she stepped back into the middle of the room. "But it's *not*. What makes it so hard is making it *look* easy. Here, watch."

Miss Emily offered her full and undivided attention as Paige hummed strains of music accompanying a series of steps and hip movements that seemed to require a rhythm completely different to that of her arms and shoulders. She indeed made it seem easy, and out of an obvious sense of accomplishment, Paige repeated the movements as precisely as she had the first time. She ended with a self-satisfied smile and looked to Miss Emily for a response.

"You look just like one of those dancers on television," she said, eyes as sincere as her compliment. "Wouldn't it be fun to see you on there one day?"

"I'm afraid I'm too old for that, Miss Em."

"Oh, no," she replied. "You must never say that."

"I don't mean that I think I'm too old to keep learning. I'm going to be like you when I'm your age—always challenging myself to learn new things, working hard, staying busy." Paige pulled over the old upholstered hassock matching Emily's chair and sat in front of her. "I just meant that being a professional dancer at this point in my life is unrealistic. That would have taken way more from me a whole lot earlier. I'm just happy I can learn what I am now and that I can help with the university show."

"How *is* your teacher, dear? She's been in my prayers every night since you told me about her."

"Oh, you should see her eyes, Miss Em; they're different, they're beautiful again. She's changed—the tone in her voice, even her gestures—I don't know how to explain it exactly, only that it seems to be all about the dance now, not about anything else. Or maybe it's me changing, I don't know. It just feels like now when Marissa shouts out directions and uses her arms and shoulders to show me things that she *wants* me to get it right—that she *expects* me to get it right. It *feels* different."

"You're both changing. You see, God is at work."

Or fate is shifting and settling the elements into harmony, but to question what makes it right in Miss Emily's mind would be *out* of the question. The result is what matters.

Emily continued, "Growth can't happen without change, but what has happened to Marissa doesn't seem to be a fair change to her life. It's hard for us to understand what growth requires that drastic of a change."

As she listened to Emily, Paige realized how easy it was to overlook the soft little-girl tone of her voice and hear the wisdom in her words. And whatever wisdom Emily had to offer, Paige would take. She listened carefully.

"But what we can't understand, we must accept on faith that it will somehow work to our good."

Learn from life's lessons how to make our lives better.

"I thought losing my Nathan would be more than I could bear. Why would God take a man who was so good to me? I didn't understand, but I learned how strong my spirit was and I realized how much I knew. I could do a lot of things for myself, and I could even help others. It was hard for a long time but it wasn't more than I could bear, and, you see, it's not more than Marissa can bear."

"You think Marissa's going to be all right."

"Just like He always sends me someone special, He sent her someone special, too."

Evan came to mind until Emily made her meaning clear. "I don't think it was only the show that you've helped."

"Me?"

"Yes, dear. Don't you see how much you've been needed?"

Of course, it was one of the reasons she'd stayed so long—for Evan, for the show. Maybe for Marissa.

"There has only been one other time in my life," she said, looking directly into Emily's eyes, "when I've been needed . . . My mother needed me."

Emily leaned forward and placed her hand on Paige's forearm. "Special," she said with a gentle pat, "like I said."

"Needed," Paige replied. "Special's a stretch."

"No, no, no," Marissa's voice rang out over the music before the room went silent and Paige spun to a stop in the middle of the dance room. "Remember your focus, straight ahead here, Paige. Your head turns last," she explained from the bench near the wall. "Do you want a break?"

"No. I'll get it this time," Paige promised. "Go ahead, start it from the beginning."

The music began again. Paige moved with the sureness and adeptness indicative of hard work and dedication. Steps and moves that once were instinctive or mimicked were now techniques with names. Raw natural ability was now harnessed into precisely timed steps and technically sound expression. She continued through the number, Marissa marking time silently now, and through the turns.

"Good. Yes!" exclaimed Marissa. "That's it, that's it!"

Paige smiled and bowed at the praise.

121

"All right," Marissa said. "You might as well learn to do that right, too." She stood from the bench with the cane she'd been using more now in place of the walker, and stepped to the end of the bench. There, she leaned the cane against the wall and proceeded slowly toward the middle of the room without it.

"Look at *you*," Paige remarked in obvious surprise.

"Never mind me," replied Marissa. "Concentrate on yourself." She positioned herself next to Paige and took her hand. "Hands here. The cast will take a group bow. The women will drop their right leg back and slightly behind the left and bend the left knee."

"Head up?"

"I like head up with a big smile." She let go of her hand and stepped back. "Again," she said, and nodded her approval as Paige complied. "All right, that's good for today. The last number is ready to go."

"We're off the clock then?"

"So to speak. Why?"

"I have a personal question."

"I don't answer personal questions."

"How long have you been walking like that without the cane?"

Paige could tell from Marissa's expression that she would answer her.

"About two weeks," she said, and added a slight little smile as she turned to head back to the bench.

"I'm really happy for you," Paige said, beside her now. "You *must* be excited."

"I try not to get too excited about things. I don't handle the let-downs very well."

"Does Evan know?"

"No."

"Anybody else know?"

Marissa turned and met Paige's eyes. "No."

Paige smiled. "You let me be the first."

Marissa broke eye contact. "It wasn't planned."

"That's okay," Paige replied, pulling a towel from her bag and wiping her face and arms. "I still feel honored." She noted another almost smile and decided to press further. "Would you celebrate and have dinner with me tonight?"

Marissa seemed genuinely surprised. "Like I said . . . Look, this doesn't mean that I'm ever going to be able to do any better than this. And I'm not going to get excited—"

"Let me get excited for you. Or, if you'd rather, help me celebrate that I learned the last of the choreography."

"The show *will* go on, that's worth celebrating."

"Seven o'clock?"

Marissa held up her hand. "Seven o'clock."

The restaurant was Marissa's choice, a well-respected bar and grill in a little community on the outskirts of Ann Arbor. The booth was large and made of old dark wood and softly lit. There was comfortable chatter all around muted by a mix of popular music and the flicker of a TV above the bar. It was their first socially exclusive time together and in Paige's mind it was perfect.

Sipping a mango margarita, Marissa looked considerably more relaxed than Paige had ever seen her. "A Diet Coke?" Marissa asked. "I thought you wanted to celebrate?"

"I don't tempt fate anymore. However number of misses you're allowed, I'm sure I've used them up."

"What fate are you afraid of?"

The worst fate she could imagine. "Becoming my mother," Paige answered.

"When it comes to family, I refuse to venture guesses. That's a fast way to send this so-far-amicable outing into something nasty."

Paige folded her hands around her glass and watched an older couple in their maize-and-blue caps make their way past the booth. "My mother's an addict," she explained. "Drugs and alcohol." She turned back to Marissa. "I guess when you're young you think you can beat any odds. Now I'm not willing to bet that it's not inherited."

123

"You keep right on surprising me, don't you?"

"Which confirms how low your opinion of me was."

Marissa held their gaze through another mango sip. "I was sure that you had the ability, but I admit I didn't believe you would be able to commit yourself to the kind of effort it takes to learn what you've learned."

Paige raised her glass over the center of the table and Marissa met her toast with a smile. "To surprises," she said.

"As long as they're good ones," Paige added. "Like you walking on your own."

Marissa placed her hand on the head of the cane hanging on the edge of the table. "I can't say that this will ever be very far from my side, but I'll do the best I can." She offered an affable tilt of her head. "I, too, worry about addiction. I promised myself that I would not become addicted to the pain-killers. With all the pain that I've experienced over my dancing career, I was sure that I could handle anything. So I stopped taking them. What I didn't understand was that part of the prescription acted to reduce inflammation. By not taking them I was actually slowing my own healing. You . . . well, you made me take a fresh look at things."

Their conversation waned only long enough to order their dinners, then Paige picked it up again. "I want to apologize for saying the things I said to you that day. I had no right—"

"No, you didn't," she said firmly. "But you were right." The little lamps on the wall cast catch lights that danced in Marissa's eyes and contradicted her tone. "Everyone else is too close to me to say the truth. You made me so angry that I cried. It was the first time that I had cried since the accident. And once I started, I couldn't stop. I hated you, first for your insolence and for your ability to dance when I can't, then for the truth. I hated God for allowing this to happen, and then I hated myself. And I knew you were right. I don't know how long I cried. I don't remember stopping. But then, there was Evan, with his tapes and his devotion, and I knew I had to try again." She leaned back in her seat. "I never thought I'd be thanking *you*. But I don't know how long it would have taken me to get to that point on my own—or if I *ever* would have."

"You would have." A desire to reassure her, to comfort her, seemed to come out of nowhere. Yet it had a familiar, almost magnetic pull that Paige couldn't resist. "I know your spirit, it wouldn't have broken."

"Before the accident I never would have believed it possible. It would have been a non-issue, unthinkable. But it did break, Paige. It scared the hell out of me."

"Your spirit wasn't broken. Even in the low places, like when Evan and I found you, it just needed time to repair."

"I'm not so sure it would have if you and Evan hadn't persisted."

Paige shook her head slowly. "It would have risen up."

"What makes you so sure? You don't know me."

Paige stared in thought. She *did* know her. She knew that her strength wasn't relative to the size of her body, that her life wouldn't be compared by that of presidents and kings, but the worth of it hadn't yet found its measuring stick. And she was sure because the familiarity had found its place.

Marissa sipped her drink in silence.

"I've seen your kind of spirit before," Paige said, "in my mother. I was too young to know what it was then. I saw the drugs and my stepfather knock it down and the alcohol dull it, but it was still there. And every once in a while the mother who had held me and sung to me and told me I was her pretty little girl would re-emerge. I know now that it was her spirit rising up."

"Did she get help?"

Paige focused on the ice cubes melting in her drink and thought about how strange it had made her feel when she had stopped at her mother's house and realized that she must still live there. She looked up to reply. "There's a song by Tracy Chapman, I've been singing it in my head for days. It asks, 'If you knew that you would be alone/Knowing right being wrong/Would you change?' The words are so personal; they ask what I've asked of myself, what I've wondered of her. It keeps asking throughout the song what would make us change. 'How bad how good does it need to get? How many losses how much regret?' It asks the questions and dares us for an answer we may never have . . . You asked me if she ever got help." Paige placed her hand on her chest. "Here in my heart she has."

It was a long moment before Marissa asked, "How long has it been since you've seen her?"

"Long enough to give up the worst of it, not too long to lose the best."

"And what was the best?"

The corners of Paige's mouth turned upwards only slightly, not a smile but a gentle indication of a memory well kept. "Her eyes," she said, staring at that distant memory. "When she was sober, and I could always tell when she was, even when I was very young, I could believe what I saw in her eyes."

Marissa, whether it was from not knowing what to say or from an innate sense of what was needed, waited patiently.

"There was love there," Paige continued, "for me. And although all the bad times made me doubt it, the very next time I saw it, I believed it all aver again."

The waitress arrived with their dinners. Marissa waited until they were alone again to respond. "I want you to know something, something I should have been able to say to you earlier, but couldn't. I *have* misjudged you, Paige. It has taken me a long time to get to the point where I can admit that much of my judgment of you had more to do with my own narrow vision of the world, my own inability to adapt and grow, than it did with who you are. I never allowed the time to get to know who you were—until now. I hope you will accept my apology for that, and for being such an arrogant ass."

"I never thought that about you. Besides, it's not the first time in my life someone has thought of me as less than admirable." She gave a little tilt of her head. "And I'm sure that it won't be the last."

"Well I'm not one of them anymore. What we shared the first time we met is in perspective now. It was what it was. It didn't call for speculation or expectation beyond what we both wanted that night. I'm able to see you now as a very caring and private person, and what you have accomplished in these past weeks *is* admirable. I want you to know that I recognize that."

Paige nodded her acceptance. "Not bad for a bar dancer?"

"Something, I *will* admit, that has its own special appeal. But that's the only admission I'm making," she said, placing her napkin on her lap.

Paige smiled to herself as Marissa concentrated on her salad. "None other needed," she replied quietly.

Chapter 26

The auditorium was a bustle of activity, one dance group leaving the stage, another finding their marks and reminding each other of positioning changes. Assistants barked out directions and Paige sat in the front row as naturally as a veteran teacher in front of her class.

Marissa stood at the back of the auditorium and breathed in the familiar smell, old wood and fabric seasoned with years of laughter and tears and impassioned hopes. She breathed it in deeply, letting it seek out the voids and bring her back to a place she had missed even more than she realized.

As the music began, she eased into an aisle seat in the back row to watch her choreography come to life. It was as she had envisioned, the right dancers, the right combination. She watched with a practiced eye through the starts and stops and jotted down notes on her clipboard. At the end of a full run-through she tucked the cane under her arm and started slowly down the aisle.

Halfway down she was noticed by one of the senior dancers. "Ms. L," she heard quickly passed around the stage. "It's Ms. L." Dancers and assistants from the back appeared on stage, resting dancers stood, and a single handclap quickly became a standing ovation as Marissa neared the first few rows. Paige, too, was standing and clapping. Then, one by one, each dancer descended the stage steps and in turn hugged and greeted their mentor.

The last assistant released her embrace. A clearly emotional Marissa wiped the tears from her face and cleared her throat. "I've missed being here more than you know. The sight of you lifts me up like nothing else can," she said, holding the clipboard over her heart. She waited appreciatively while cheers erupted and subsided, then added, "Now go back to work and make Ms. Flemming proud."

"Well, look at you," Paige said quietly as Marissa took the seat next to her.

"You just concentrate on your dancers."

She ignored Paige's smile and handed her the clipboard and its page of notes.

The rest of the rehearsal consisted of Paige taking Marissa's corrections on stage and making sure each one translated into perfect execution. The partnership worked surprisingly well and Marissa found herself watching Paige in a whole new light. The detachment that had characterized weeks of teaching and practice had given way to a more personal scrutiny.

She watched Paige interacting, demonstrating, smiling now and then. She was precise and careful, following directions exactly. There was no stepping beyond her bounds and trying to do more than she was capable of. Respectful, smart—two words she never thought she'd attribute to Paige Flemming. Funny how the unexpected always seems to be the most humbling.

Paige had dismissed the last of the dancers and rejoined Marissa. "What do you think overall?" she asked.

Marissa finished a note to herself and responded, "It's coming along very well. A few things we'll talk about changing, but you're doing a good job, Paige, a really good job."

"Thank you. I want to do the best job I can for you. I know this show means a lot."

"I lost track of just how much for a while there. I'm thankful that Evan didn't." She grasped the railing in front of the seats and pulled herself up. "Speaking of Evan," she said, "did he give you the forms to fill out for the university?"

Page nodded. "I already gave them back to him."

"You're not salaried, so you have to be paid like an independent contractor. You're responsible for reporting the earnings on your tax return."

"I know, I've had to do that before. I don't usually make enough for Uncle Sam to take a bite, but I always let him know that."

"Good," she said and tucked the cane under her arm.

"How did you get here today?"

"A cab."

Paige grabbed her bag and keys. "Let me drive you home then."

"It's not necessary, Paige."

"Actually, it would give me a chance to pass something by you about the 'Time of My Life' number."

"Yes," Marissa agreed, "that's one I wanted to change."

Paige dropped her bag next to the bench in Marissa's dance room. "This is what I had in mind," she said, quickly moving to the middle of the room.

Marissa settled onto the bench and watched her.

"As you noticed, Jon is having a hard time with the transition from here," she moved through the steps and stopped, "through the turn," she continued into the turn, "and the reconnect with Vanessa."

Marissa was nodding.

"What if we start him here," she moved back three steps from the original starting position. "And," she moved through the steps again, "let him make the turn to the left for the reconnect." She finished and stopped. "I've seen him do that turn in warm-ups and it's so smooth."

"But then you have to adjust Vanessa's steps," she said, starting toward the middle of the floor.

"Are you sure?" Paige asked. "We aren't adding any steps, only moving the starting point."

"Start over there," Marissa directed, "and run through Vanessa's part from the turn back toward center." She watched as the routine brought Paige to a spot only a step away from her own

130

position. "Okay," Marissa said, "I'll take Vanessa's position, and you run through Jon's steps just as you proposed."

Arms positioned precisely, Marissa waited as Paige traveled the proposed change, and smiled as she sailed past her outstretched hand with no possibility of reconnecting.

Hands on her hips, Paige turned back to face Marissa, offered a humble smile and wrinkled her nose.

"That's okay," Marissa said. "Don't forget I've been doing this since 1875." She got the laugh she was after and added, "We can make it work, and I think we should. Normally, I make them learn the choreography because it's part of their performing experience. But we got a late start and this is minor in the grand scheme of things. Here," she said taking Paige's hand, "hold your last position."

She released her hand and walked slowly to a spot she calculated in her head. From there she turned and with painstaking deliberation, Marissa walked through the movements until she stopped just inches short of Paige's hand. She changed places with Paige and said, "Do the steps from here back. Then repeat them back to me."

The calculation was good and Paige ended in the correct position. Marissa changed places again and directed, "This time take Jon's part right through the tempo change."

"With the music?"

"Sure."

Paige started the music and took her position.

Statuesque—a description not many would question, Marissa decided, watching Paige wait for the musical cue. Roman nose and deep-set eyes, strong features for a woman, but decidedly not masculine. And there was something else she had grown to appreciate over the past weeks, an expression, a look of total concentration that at first brought a smile to Marissa's face. Now she knew what it could produce; now it was endearing.

Paige snapped into motion right on cue and seconds later had taken Marissa's outstretched hand and pulled her into a turn that, at the tempo change, should have put her in an embrace with her back against Paige's chest. Instead, it pulled Marissa off-balance and nearly dropped her to the floor before Paige could catch her and hold her up.

"Oh, God, Marissa. I'm sorry, I'm sorry." She held her steady until Marissa could get her footing, then lifted her upright.

"I'm fine Paige. Just a little embarrassed, that's all." She clung to Paige's arms long enough to assure her balance, and then longer because she liked how it felt.

"You're incredible," Paige said softly. "You have no reason to be embarrassed."

It didn't matter if it was the compliment or the softness of her tone, the feeling she had now was a little too good. Marissa released her grasp. "Let me prove that I can at least stand on my own feet," she said. "Will you try it again for me?"

"You must trust me more than I'm trusting myself."

Marissa tilted her head. The good feeling stayed as long as she looked into the charming blue of Paige's eyes. "The music please?"

Paige complied, resetting the music and taking the position once again. On cue she traveled the distance to Marissa's hand and this time pulled her safely into an embrace. The tempo slowed, they swayed to the count—one, two, three—one rhythm, one body. Movements giving the music vision and feel and warmth. It was what Marissa had experienced for years and what, in this moment, Paige was allowing her to feel once again.

She was aware, however, that it was more than the music she felt. The warmth went beyond the heat of the dance. It went beyond the heat of Paige's body pressed tightly against her own, and beyond the breath passing over the flush of her cheek. It came from an appeal she hadn't expected. Certainly on some order the appeal was physical, added to an unexplainable understanding of who this woman really was. But more than anything, it came from respect. It took humility and damn hard work to do what Paige had done. More than that, it took doing it for someone else. For me.

The push away and pull back had put them face to face, bodies barely touching, the music demanding she lift her focus to Paige's eyes. When she did, Paige's hand came to her cheek as the chore-ography called for. It did not call for the twinge of excitement it caused, or for Marissa to bring her lips so close to Paige's, or for the music to go on without them.

When Paige left the decision to Marissa, it was an easy one to make—easier than words. She kissed Paige tenderly, a silent thank you that lingered in the softness. A gentle give and take that ended when Marissa decided it should. Her lips, though, stayed close and her heart refused to slow its beat as she whispered, "Thank you."

Paige waited for Marissa's eyes, then seemed to search them for something before replying, "For not dropping you this time?"

Marissa slid her arms around Paige's waist. "You know what for," she said, as Paige embraced her. "And it doesn't matter why."

"Because you're incredible," Paige whispered into the damp hair over Marissa's temple.

"*That* I'm not sure I could ever claim." Marissa eased from their embrace, keeping a hand on Paige's arm until she was sure of her balance. She had pushed the last dose of medication further than she had intended.

"It's time that you kick me out of here now," Paige said, "and get some rest."

"Now you're reading my mind."

Paige followed close behind her as Marissa made her way to the bench. "No, just common sense. You've had a long day. Is there anything I can do for you before I leave?"

Marissa looked up from her seat on the bench. "No, but thank you. Tomorrow, though," she added as Paige picked up her bag. "Would you pick me up for rehearsal?"

Paige swung the bag over her shoulder and smiled. "You bet."

Chapter 27

Jack hadn't stopped the car yet in Geri's drive before she was out the side door, large canvas bag in tow, and on her way to the passenger's side door.

"Hi, Bradley," she said, placing the bag in the back next to his car seat. She pulled out a little board with a jungle scene on it and animal magnets lined up at the bottom and handed it to him. "I brought a game for you to play while we're in the car."

He gave the board only a passing look and said excitedly, "We're going to see the pandas."

"Yes," she replied, quickly sliding into the front seat. She turned her head to smile at him. "Thank you for letting me go with you boys."

Bradley dropped the board onto the seat beside him without a second look. "We have to hurry, Popu."

Jack laughed and winked at Geri. "We're just not moving fast *enough* for that boy . . . We're on our way," he directed at Bradley. "We're not going to miss them."

He backed the car out of the drive before explaining. "He heard Jackie tell me that the pandas are on loan to the zoo and they're only going to be there for another month. Of course, if you're four a month might just as well be an hour."

Once they were on their way Jack reached across the console and took Geri's hand. "I promised Jackie a Saturday to take them, but she hasn't been able to get a Saturday off. Low on the totem pole." He looked over and squeezed Geri's hand. "I'm glad you wanted to spend the day with us."

"I've never been to a zoo," she said, catching his eye. Then, lowering her voice, she said, "And it's been a real long time since I've spent any time with little ones."

"You'll be fine," he reassured her. "It's like riding a bike."

"I never learned to ride that bike."

Another squeeze of her hand. "You'll do fine."

The whole process of parking the car, walking half the length of the parking lot, and then waiting in line for tickets was almost beyond Bradley's tolerance. He tugged at Jack's hand, wanting him to run, and asked half a dozen times if he knew where the pandas were.

Once inside the gate, Jack found the first available bench and sat down to study the map so that they could make their way to the pandas first. Any attempt to see anything else first would be disastrous, Jack knew, so while Bradley danced and fidgeted and craned his neck to see if he could see them, Jack found the quickest path, put Bradley on his shoulders and headed out at as brisk a pace as possible. Geri, tote bag in hand, stayed close to Jack's side as they worked their way through the meandering crowd.

From his eagle's-nest perch, Bradley saw them first. "Popu, I see them," he shouted, his voice hitting an ecstatic octave, his hands hitting the top of Jack's head. "I see 'em, I see 'em!"

His excitement was contagious. Geri beamed up a bright smile and Jack quickened his step.

"I'll bet I'm gonna be glad I insisted on pull-ups for today. With all this jumpin' around up here," he turned stiff-necked toward Geri, "I can tell you now them pants ain't dry."

Geri cut her laugh short to exclaim, "I see them, too, Jack! Oh, they're beautiful . . . Aren't they beautiful, Bradley?"

Bradley was awestruck. Atop Jack's shoulders, in the first open space at the fence, he stared wide-eyed and open-mouthed at his black-and-white obsession.

They stood at the fence for over half an hour while the two bears rolled and frolicked and munched on shoots of bamboo. Bradley hadn't moved once or uttered a word the entire time. His hands, clamped tightly onto Jack's hair, only loosened their grip when the bears tired of their play and disappeared behind a wall of rock.

Someone nearby said, "I think they're off to take a nap," and Jack took that as his cue to head for the nearest available bench.

Bradley never took his eyes from the spot where the bears disappeared, turning his head to its limit, then snapping it around quickly in the opposite direction to regain his surveillance.

Jack lifted his grandson from his shoulders with a groan and placed him on the bench next to Geri. "I guess I *am* getting old," he said, tousling Bradley's hair and taking a seat next to him. "I remember carrying mine on my shoulders all day long when they were little." He shook his head. "It was worth it though, even if I am whipped. I just wish I could have seen his face."

"I'm going to wait for them to wake up," Bradley announced, heading for a spot at the fence again.

"Okay," Jack called after him, "but you stay right there where we can see you."

"His face was precious," Geri told him. "What I saw of it anyway. I was pretty busy watching the pandas myself. I never realized how big they are."

The look on her face made Jack smile. "I think you're going to enjoy today almost as much as Bradley." He put his arm around her shoulders and pulled her toward him to place a kiss on her cheek. "Let's see if we can talk him into seeing some other animals while we wait for the pandas to come back out."

It took some time, but watching the video about the pandas in their natural habitat and repeated promises to return when the bears were out again finally convinced Bradley to help Jack show Geri the other animals.

They worked their way around to see all of the big cats and then on to the giant tortoises, all of which held Bradley's interest surprisingly well. But Jack wasn't about to press his luck.

"Hey, I don't know about you two," he said as they neared a food court, "but I'm starting to get hungry."

"Oh," Geri replied, pointing to the canvas bag Jack had been carrying for her. "I packed sandwiches. They're in a little cooler pack."

"Well, that sounds good to me. How 'bout some lunch, buddy?"

They claimed an empty table, but Bradley wasn't ready to settle yet. He circled the table and looked toward the food stands until he spotted it. "Hot dogs! There, Popu. Can I have a hot dog?"

It was hard to deny such a tempting request. Jack looked at Geri and gave her a "geez, you know what I really want" look.

"That's okay," she said. "Go get hot dogs for you guys. The sandwiches will keep until later."

It was the response Jack needed, the one that showed she understood. He hurried off with a still-happy grandson to get hot dogs and drinks.

He was pleased with himself so far. The first half of the day had been a complete success. The midday, after-lunch melt down, though, was bound to happen. Four-year-old stamina wasn't even up to par with granddad stamina, a fact Jack was well aware of. He headed for the penguin enclosure with trepidation.

"I think he has to go to the bathroom," Geri offered as discreetly as possible. An effort lost by Bradley's tight grip on the front of his pants.

Jack picked him up. "You forget to tell Popu something? Let's find a bathroom before we have to change those pull-ups again."

But getting to the bathroom was only half the battle. Once back on the ground, Bradley stood defiantly outside the entrance. "I can do it by myself."

"I know you can," Jack replied. "But we're not at home. Do you remember why we have the rule for public bathrooms?"

He clung to the front of his pants and crossed his legs. "I wanna do it by myself."

Jack took hold of Bradley's free hand. "Come on before you pee your pants."

"Nooo," Bradley whined, pulling his hand away.

"Do you want me to take you in with me?" Geri offered.

"No," he said with a sharp turn of his head.

Jack crouched down in front of him. He spoke in a soft, low voice that indicated that the conversation was just between the two of them. "I know you want Geri to see what a big boy you are, so, let's make a deal. You go on in there and take care of business by yourself and I'll stand just around the corner of that wall there, between the bathroom and the outside. See from right there I can look in and see the whole bathroom, so I'll know what stall you go into. And if I'm standing *there,* Geri can see me and she'll know that I'm not helping you." He ventured a quick glance Geri's way to see her attempt at looking disinterested. "We got a deal?"

Bradley nodded and turned quickly toward the bathroom.

"I wonder if *I* would have had the good sense to figure that out," Geri mused once they finally stood before the penguin enclosure. "You're a good dad, Jack, a good granddad."

"Oh, I made my share of mistakes along the way. Sometimes I wonder how I got so lucky to have my kids turn out so good. I look back and see things that I wish I *had* had the good sense to handle differently."

"Like what?"

"My second boy," he began, "there was a time with him I surely wish I had back again." He turned from the glass wall to face Geri. "He had just turned sixteen, got his driver's license, earned a few privileges. I'd never had a problem with my first boy not coming home on time or telling me where he was. But Darren, he was different. So, about the third time he'd come in late I grounded him. Took the driving privileges away for a month. Of course it had to be a month when everything was going on at school, and he ended up jumpin' in a car with a bunch of friends and late that night I got a phone call I'll never forget. They'd been in an accident, no seatbelts, and four of the five kids were in the hospital. Darren was one of them. Every one of them made it outta that mess with their lives, but no amount of surgery could make Darren's right leg normal again. We'll both have to live with that decision for the rest of our lives."

"But you did what you thought was best. You tried to keep him safe."

Jack nodded. "That I did. But even when you think you're making the right decision, things can get all turned around and end up in a way you never thought they would."

"No perfect parents, huh?"

"Nope, no such thing."

It wasn't long before the penguin antics and even their swimming so close to the glass weren't enough to hold Bradley's attention. He began to fidget, rubbing his eyes and his hair and shifting his weight from foot to foot. His words came out as a soft whine. "I wanna see the pandas."

Jack took his hand. "Okay," he said, "we'll head back over there."

Soon Bradley's pace slowed considerably, then he stopped in the middle of the walkway.

"You're getting tired, aren't you?" Jack asked.

"No," Bradley replied with a vigorous shake of his head. "I'm *not* tired. I'm thirsty."

Geri reached inside the canvas bag. "Here, look. I brought a bottle of water just for you." She retrieved the bottle and quickly pulled the plastic covering off the pop-up top.

"Nooo," Bradley whined, bouncing up and down and reaching for the bottle. "I wanna do it." He grabbed the bottle from Geri and offered her only an ungrateful-looking scowl and another whine that sounded suspiciously close to crying.

"Okay, that *is* enough." Jack couched once again in front of his grandson. "You *are* tired, mister. Look at Popu." He waited for Bradley to lift his eyes. "It's okay to be tired. Popu's tired, too. But it's not okay to be rude to Geri. She was thinking about you when she gave you that bottle of water. So what do you say?"

Bradley lowered his head and turned toward Geri. A couple of seconds passed before he lifted his head. The scowl was gone. "Thank you for the water."

"You're very welcome, honey."

"Now I'll bet you can open the rest of that top by yourself,"

Jack said. "And then we're gonna take a break over there in the shade so that Popu and Geri can rest."

The cool shade of the tree and the chance to rest on a bench with a back was overdue. "Ahhh," Jack sighed. "This feels good."

Bradley sat between them, still sipping from the bottle and snapping the top open and closed.

Geri smiled wearily. "So, this is what I missed with mine?"

Jack chuckled. "Well, yeah, there mighta been a plus side there."

Bradley handed the bottle to Jack and without a word he curled his legs up on the bench, reached his arm around Geri's waist and laid his head on her lap.

She looked hesitantly at Jack, then at the little body curled around her before she allowed herself to drop her arm around him. "And a lot that I shouldn't have missed," she said, stroking her fingers carefully through the soft brown hair.

He watched her as her posture softened and wondered if her reservations were gone, if she knew now that it was only the alcohol that had kept her from being the parent that she could have been. There's no ideal, it doesn't exist. You just do the best you can. She would've done better, without the alcohol. He wanted her to know that.

Maybe that's what today was for—for her. Not for himself, because he liked spending time with her, or because he was beginning to have reasons beyond the case, beyond Ann, to be with her. He had to believe that it was for her because there had to be justification that he could believe in when he put the last piece of the puzzle together, when he had to leave and bring Ann in. There had to be justification beyond his duty to his job for him to spend this kind of time with her. Otherwise, how could he in good conscience keep doing this knowing that he would end up breaking her heart? There had to be something in this for her besides a broken heart.

Lately it was all he could do to keep his thoughts straight. He had to remind himself of his purpose during those times when it became clouded with Geri's needs, his own needs. She was beginning to love him, to count on his presence, he could feel it. She was careful not to say it, but the more time they spent together the more obvious it was.

The thought that had become more prevalent of late was that he had done all he could do to solve the case—a case with no leads in all these years, no DNA evidence except the victim's, and despite time and opportunity, no indication that Geri knew anything that could help him. Maybe there would never be a clue to follow, a piece of the puzzle that would fall into place that disclosed the whole picture. The possibility that he had been unwilling to even consider until now was that this case may not be solvable. And if that was the reality of it . . .

Jack pressed his cheek to the top of Geri's head as she snuggled against his shoulder. Maybe it *is* time to let go of it, time to pursue something more real.

Chapter 28

It had become a routine in itself—Paige picking Marissa up after work, the two of them working the rehearsal together, then spending the evening together either at a restaurant or at Marissa's. They were good evenings, two weeks of them, some with Evan and some alone, each filled with work discussions and laughter. Tonight the three of them shared homemade burritos and *The Graduate*.

Evan reached the remote from his nest in a pile of pillows on the floor. "I can't believe she's gone," he said. "I've got this obsession of going to see every Anne Bancroft movie there is, one right after the other."

"Not tonight, I hope," Marissa quipped. She flexed first one leg then the other from atop the pillow on Paige's lap.

"Are you feeling okay?" Paige asked.

Marissa nodded and stretched both legs straight.

Paige tried for eye contact but Marissa avoided it. "Half a dose is wearing off?" She knew without Marissa answering.

"I just overdid it."

"It keeps the inflammation down, remember?" Paige insisted carefully. "Just a little so that you can sleep tonight?"

At Marissa's nod, Paige slipped from beneath the pillow and left the room. Marissa ignored Evan's smile and repositioned herself at the end of the couch with the pillow behind her back. "So, how many movies are we talking?" "Oh, God," he replied. "She starred in over fifty films—*The Miracle Worker, Pumpkin Eater, Agnes of God, Garbo Talks*," he motioned toward Marissa, "*The Turning Point*. She earned awards up the wazoo—Academy, Golden Globes, British Academy, National Board of Review—Emmys. God, so talented."

Marissa accepted the medication and water from Paige and downed it quickly. "She was fantastic in *The Turning Point*," she agreed. "Such an excellent movie in so many ways."

"Have you seen it, Paige?" Evan asked.

"No. What's it about?"

"Two friends—" Marissa began.

"Dancers," Evan interjected.

"Who make different life decisions and have to face the doubts about whether they had made the right decision. Years later, when the two friends are face to face, they're forced to deal with their envy of each other's decision. Both were talented dancers, one chose to give up her chance at a dance career for marriage and a family. The other chose to dedicate herself to what it took to be a famous dancer. It's a movie that hits home."

"And which," Evan jumped to his feet, "is tomorrow night's movie entertainment." He grabbed his keys from the table and lifted his jacket from the chair. "Chinese okay for tomorrow? I'm buying."

"You don't have to make that offer twice," Marissa replied.

"I didn't think so," he winked. "See you ladies tomorrow."

He let himself out and Paige began picking up the empty glasses from the table. "I should get going, too," she said, "so you can get some sleep."

She returned from the kitchen and leaned to kiss Marissa goodnight. As she stood to leave, Marissa took her hand and looked directly into her eyes.

"Have you ever doubted an important decision, Paige? One that essentially formed the rest of your life?"

The seriousness of the question surprised her at first. Paige kept hold of Marissa's hand and sat next to her. It obviously came from thoughts of the movie she hadn't seen, but that was not an excuse for not answering it. "Yes," she heard herself saying, "I have." An admission she had made to no one, one she had tried not to dwell on. "But after so much time, what good does thinking on it now do? There's no going back."

"Of course not, but maybe reflection will lead to enlightenment."

"What choice do you doubt?" Paige asked.

"The most?"

Paige raised her eyebrows. "More than one?"

"Oh, many, if I'm honest." Marissa frowned in thought. "How do you decide what's important in life? And does it change?"

"This is obviously bothering you tonight. I wish you were talking with someone smarter than I am."

Marissa squeezed Paige's hand. "You're smarter than you know. I wish you would stay and talk with me. Please."

"For whatever it's worth, then, I'm here until you kick me out."

Marissa's eyes were fiercely fixed on Paige. "See, I wonder if I really decided what was important, or if I merely followed some instinctual path—because it felt right at the time. And, if I am a creature of instinct rather than thought, have I fixated so hard on that path that I couldn't listen to an instinct that might have changed my course?"

Paige hesitated at the thought that she would sound stupid, then decided to risk it. "Whether we make decisions from thought or instinct, either one can get overridden by everyday living. It's hard enough to keep sight of the path when all those daily tasks and decisions crowd over the top of it. I wonder how much time anyone spends plotting their life course, or changing it." She knew she hadn't given any great revelation. "Are you questioning whether it took the accident to change a course that you wouldn't have changed on your own?"

"Yes, I am."

"Whew. Why didn't you just say that?"

The seriousness that had furrowed Marissa's brow disappeared almost instantaneously. "I *like* to wear myself out."

Paige's laugh was not only spontaneous, it was contagious.

At the end of a much-needed laugh, Marissa asked, "And you? A creature of thought, or instinct?"

"Clearly instinct," she replied. "For me, thought seems to follow the driven path." Marissa's eyes hadn't left hers. They studied in silence. Not ready to talk about her path or what drove it, Paige waited without an answer or a polite way out if Marissa asked.

But Marissa didn't ask. She dropped her eyes to Paige's lips and leaned forward into a kiss. This was not the kiss that had wished goodnight or said thank you over the past two weeks. This kiss heated with its touch, parted and invited, and asked only one question.

Paige's answer was to pull Marissa into an embrace and return her kiss with the intensity it deserved. And, she hoped, with the intensity Marissa expected. The desire had been there all along. The decision to act on it, however, had to be Marissa's, because unlike before, this time she *needed* to be desired. To not show her that she was desirable was not an option. She must not think that scars or physical limitations made her any less desirable.

She felt the warmth of Marissa's body in her arms, the rapid heartbeat against her chest. Lips, warm and soft and wet, moved against her own. Paige tasted them with her tongue, heard the soft moan in reply. "I've wanted to do this," she whispered, brushing it over Marissa's lips, "since I first saw you again."

"What took you so long?" came the whispered reply.

Paige held her lips away. "I thought you hated me."

"I did," she said, closing the gap to kiss Paige firmly and deeply.

This time it wasn't the frenzied groping, racing to catch desire before it exploded. This time there was time, as much time as they needed, as much as they wanted. So Paige took her time— stroking silk auburn hair and fine creamy skin, kissing the tender places on her neck, inhaling the scent of her—so much of what she had missed before.

Marissa was compliant in her arms, undemanding, sensual. Paige loved the feel of her, the way she moved gently into each kiss, each touch, as though she was enjoying every second. Paige listened to the cues, she felt them, the responses that said "yes, that's wonderful," "here again," "stay here longer." Following them was the easiest way she knew to let Marissa know how much she wanted to please her.

And it seemed that Marissa knew. She smiled at Paige's touch, her cheeks flushed with warmth. Her eyes sparkled, not with the coyness of their first encounter, but with what Paige loosely interpreted as appreciation. The reason for Marissa's desire this time had reached beyond the boundary of sexual gratification. For Paige, knowing that brought a whole new dimension to what they were about to experience.

"You don't have to say anything," Marissa whispered. "I don't expect anything past tonight."

"I want to be able to tell you how wonderful I think you are."

Marissa pressed her finger over Paige's lips. "Shh," she said, then replaced it with a kiss.

It was the permission Paige needed, permission to feel, permission to show it. Her hands found the slender waist, and moved smoothly around and over her back, dancer-tight beneath the thin material of Marissa's blouse.

Marissa closed their embrace with her arms around Paige's shoulders, her kisses deep and intense. The foreplay not of dance after dance of grinding hips, but this time more intimate, where parts of their souls had dared to touch each other.

The concern of worthiness, the one plaguing Paige's mind from the first moment she met Marissa, had, at least for now, disappeared. Without it there was nothing that could keep her from what was most important tonight. What Marissa wanted, what she needed, would be Paige's sole concern.

Their lips parted slightly, enough for Marissa to say softly, "I promise not to order you out of my bedroom this time."

"Is that an invitation?"

Marissa slowly rose from the couch and offered her hand to

Paige. "Don't be afraid. It doesn't look like it did the last time you saw it."

Paige took her hand. "I won't be paying any attention to your bedroom."

"One promise," Marissa said, folding back the bed covers in the darkened room, "no lights."

Paige wrapped her arms around the narrow waist from behind and kissed the regal curve of Marissa's neck. "I don't have to see you to know how beautiful you are."

Marissa pressed back against her, closed her eyes and folded her own arms over Paige's. "Keep whispering your lies and I'll pretend to believe them."

She snugged her arms and pressed her lips to the tender skin at the place where Marissa's neck met her collarbone. "Mm, no. I'll tell you no lies."

The warmth greeting her hand as it began the caress across Marissa's abdomen and down her thigh told her it wasn't going to matter if she believed her or not, not tonight anyway.

"It's no lie," Paige said softly, "that when you look at me I lose track of who I am."

Marissa stretched her hand up to caress the side of Paige's face. "Who you are," she replied, "is why I'm here with your arms around me."

Paige breathed her words softly between kisses to Marissa's face and neck. "You might have to remind me of that now and then." She felt the presence of a smile against her cheek and gave her hands the freedom to slide beneath the bottom of the untucked blouse. They were welcomed by a flush of heat and quickened breath, signs Paige easily read as the beginning of desire. "It's not a lie that all I want right now is to slide inside you."

With a quiet moan, Marissa turned in Paige's arms and kissed her. It was the kiss of a lover, open and wet, meant to spark the smoldering fire.

And it did. It quickened the spread of heat that soon enveloped

Paige's body and served to center what thought there was on one goal, pleasing Marissa in every way that she could.

Her movements were slow and deliberate, unbuttoning Marissa's blouse, slipping it from her shoulders. Paige placed gentle kisses over the smooth, warm skin of Marissa's neck and shoulders as her fingers circled the narrow waist to find the closure of Marissa's pants.

"Let's get you on the bed," she offered. "You've been standing long enough."

Marissa eased onto the bed, allowing Paige to remove the rest of her clothing. Then she reached for Paige's shirt. "How fast can you get rid of this?"

"There was a time when it would have taken the right music and five minutes for this to come off." She began unbuttoning her shirt. "But I'm not drinking like that anymore."

"And I'm not waiting five minutes, either," Marissa returned softly, "to have my hands on you."

Paige immediately shed her clothes. "No, you're not." She slipped onto the bed next to her and felt Marissa's hand first on her hip, then finding its way upward to her breast. "I'm already sorry," she whispered close to Paige's lips, "that I made you promise no lights." Her hand continued to caress Paige's breast, brushing gently over her nipple, and moving to the other. "I think you're even more beautiful than I imagined."

The caresses circled and explored, and then the warmth of Marissa's mouth, closing over her nipple, sent sensations that quickly changed the direction of Paige's desire. She lay back with a moan. "My intent was to please *you*."

"Ohh," Marissa breathed between Paige's breasts, "you are." She cupped Paige's breasts, one then the other, and visited each in turn to take the raised nipple in her mouth. She sucked them and ran her tongue over and around them.

Paige lifted her chest tighter to Marissa's mouth, encouraging the sensations that were racing to melt desire out of her control. The thought of selfishness, accepting her own satisfaction first and foremost, was a fleeting one.

Marissa was seeing to it. Her hand followed the flow of heat across Paige's abdomen as if she knew she had sent it there. And Paige could find no logic to stop the trail of kisses over her chest and neck, or to halt the path of Marissa's hand, baiting her anticipation as it moved over her hip and buttock and down her thigh.

"I like your dancer's butt, your dancer's legs," Marissa drew the words hotly against the flat plane of Paige's abdomen. "I like how you move." Silken ends of auburn hair swept over the flushed skin as Marissa moved to whisper close to Paige's ear, "I like who you are."

Whether it was the validation of the words that caused the gasp of air that Paige couldn't control, or Marissa's fingers clipping through the wetness she'd caused, Paige couldn't tell. Nor did it matter; the feeling was so close, so good.

Paige laced her fingers through Marissa's hair and brought their lips together in a kiss that said what words could not. She wanted her now, just as she was taking Marissa's tongue deep and full, needed her as urgently as the sounds she uttered.

Her hips began a deliberate cadence, moving into the strokes of Marissa's hand. It was a primitive rhythm, unrefined and raw, driven by need, fueled by desire. It increased with intensity, stroke after stroke, until she could no longer hold Marissa's lips, could no longer keep any thought or control. Her need was audible, her hips reaching and pressing until Marissa slid inside.

"Yes," Paige gasped, "oh, God, yes." She grasped Marissa's hand and drove her hips hard, taking the fingers deep. Again and again, until she shouted a release that exploded and rocked her body with spasms. Glorious spasms gripped her and pleased her. They left her legs quivering, her heart still pounding its rapid pulse.

Marissa lovingly kissed the firmness of Paige's thigh and hip, and placed kisses over the warm, flushed flesh as she moved upward to rest her head on Paige's chest. "You," she said softly, "are a very sexy woman."

Paige drew her arms around the slender body. "You are very

149

good at making me feel that I am." She pressed her lips to the top of Marissa's head. "Exactly what I had wanted to do for you."

Marissa snuggled into their embrace with a sigh. "Mm, will it wait until morning? Tonight I want to stay right here and fall asleep in your arms."

"It'll keep," Paige whispered. She closed her eyes. Her body began to relax. She would stay until morning and listen for the voice of warning that she knew love had once again silenced. And this time, for as long as it was silent she would allow herself to stay.

Chapter 29

"As many different parts of the country as I've seen in the fall," Paige said, stopping the car at a Dixboro intersection, "Michigan is one of the most beautiful."

Marissa looked from front to side, taking in the changes to the tiny community just north of Ann Arbor. "I don't have a lot to compare it to. Most of the country I traveled I saw from the window of an airplane. I haven't been out *here* in years."

"It's worth it," Paige returned, "if for no other reason than to see this one tree. And it's a perfect day to see it, peak color change and a sunny, cloudless sky." The light changed green. "It's right up here."

They passed what looked like an old country store, now a small antiques business, old country houses with railed porches, and turned onto a little street into an old residential neighborhood. And there it stood, on a big corner lot by itself, a large maple, its leaves a fireball of yellow-orange ablaze in the bright sun.

"Oh, it *is* beautiful, Paige! Nearly as bright as the sun itself." She sent a sly glance in Paige's direction. "And I thought the brightest thing in your life was the light strip above a bar."

"I'm just full of surprises." Paige stopped the car on the side of the road so that they could both admire the majesty of the tree. "Prettier than a postcard," she said, peering through the windshield.

Marissa lowered the window and focused a small digital camera. She took two shots of the tree before turning and snapping a picture of Paige.

She turned her head too late to avoid the picture. "What are you doing?"

"Recording the pretty things in my life right now."

Paige gazed into the gray-blue eyes and replied seriously, "I don't think I've ever been a pretty thing in anyone's life."

"Yes, you were." Marissa took Paige's hand. "You were your mother's pretty little girl."

"That was such a long tome ago. I don't remember if it felt this good."

Marissa stared silently for a few seconds, then said, "I think I believe you."

"Well," Paige started the car, "let's see how convincing a picnic and a color tour of Hudson Mills Park can be."

Moni had been right, the park was perfect, in peak color with every shade and combination of reds and yellows and oranges, and with miles of river and roads to explore. A perfect suggestion for a perfect Sunday afternoon.

Paige pulled another still-warm cinnamon donut from the bag and handed it to Marissa, then refilled their cups with cider.

"I needed this," Marissa said from her camp chair at the end of the picnic table. "Oh," she held up the donut, "not this third, absolutely sinful donut. *Today*, I really needed this kind of *day*."

"When was the last time you blew everything else off and did something that Marissa needed?"

She took a deep breath of autumn air with a faint scent of burning hickory, and scanned their little niche beside the river. "I think it was a night out with the girls about four years ago."

"Is that right?"

Marissa tilted her head to one side. "You seem to be a problem for me."

"*That's* a label I've worn before."

"Was it accurate?"

"It depends on who you ask—and who you believe."

"I know without asking how Moni and Katherine feel," Marissa said. "What if I asked your father? You've never mentioned your father."

"I don't know who he is." Then she added before Marissa could ask, "I'd rather not know, that way he can be anybody I want him to be—and that's changed over the years, depending on what I needed him to be—a politician protecting his image, a married man protecting his marriage and family, a nice man who just made a stupid decision. So, you can see what you might hear from him." Then, uncharacteristically, she added, "But my step-father . . ."

Marissa waited but it seemed Paige would say no more. "The tone of your voice tells me enough, Paige."

Grateful for the reprieve, Paige looked up. "You wouldn't have wanted to ask him."

"No," Marissa agreed. "More appropriately, I would want to ask your last lover."

Paige dropped her focus to the worn gray wood of the picnic table. Are they lovers if you only spent a night with them, or an afternoon, or an hour? What makes them a lover? "My last sex partner?"

"You see a difference?"

Not comfortable thinking aloud, Paige sorted her thoughts silently.

"Personally, I never really considered the difference," Marissa admitted.

"Was I your lover four years ago?" Paige asked.

Her expression indicated that the question had caught her off guard, but Marissa answered quickly, "No."

"Because it was just sex."

"I didn't want to think about it like that. It seems like such a male thing."

"And now, how do you think of me?"

Marissa answered directly. "As a lover."

"Because we've been making love every night?"

"Yes," she said, "and because it's more than sex. There's a lot of emotion involved." She held Paige's gaze for the next few seconds before adding, "That said, it does open the possibility of sleeping with someone one time and considering them a lover. Something you've experienced?"

"Yes, I have," Paige replied.

"I guessed as much. So, who should I ask, your last lover or your last sex partner?"

Paige almost smiled. "Neither."

"What *is* it that I'd hear from your last lover?"

"You're not going to let this drop, are you?"

"Oh, no."

"Even though it takes me to an uncomfortable place?" Paige stared into unyielding eyes. Poetic justice? Time to testify to the discomfort I've caused others. And my last lover? There had been no one since Moni she could call a lover, not until now.

Paige rubbed the back of her neck. Marissa waited patiently. Finally, Paige put the words together. "You would hear how emotional pain turned trust and love into anger." She took a deep breath and rephrased it. "No, you would hear how much someone trusted me and cared about me, and how although I knew that, I was so selfish I slept with her knowing that I would leave and hurt her."

She watched for the expression on Marissa's face to change, waited for what she expected to see there—disappointment, disdain, even disgust. A look that said "I knew you were a piece of work." But nothing changed. Marissa's face still held the same open, accepting expression. This isn't right. It's not normal. When you finally own up to your sins, you don't go unpunished. You pay for them, don't you? If I'm ready to own up, I'm ready to pay.

"Thank you," Marissa said quietly, "for telling me that."

But Paige wasn't through purging herself. "When I was younger I thought I was really good at two things, fucking and dancing. As I got older I realized that I was *only* good at those two things. Now, I know that what I am really good at is turning something beautiful and pure into something very ugly. And I don't think I can blame it on heredity."

Marissa still looked undaunted. "Do you need to blame it on anything? Maybe you just have to understand it."

"I do understand it, Marissa. I know why. What may never happen is for anyone else to understand it."

"Try me," she said.

"I can't do that." Paige leaned forward and took Marissa's hands. "Not right now. It isn't fair, but *that's* what I need you to understand."

"Just keep in mind that you're asking this of someone whose own relationship skills are trying to crash-course out of infancy."

"I don't expect any more than I am capable of giving."

Marissa's brows pushed into a frown. "You are an enigma, Paige Flemming."

A smile lifted the corners of Paige's mouth. Enigma had been in last week's crossword puzzle.

Chapter 30

The station was bustling with a higher than normal amount of energy. The police chief had the phone in one ear and detectives in and out of the office talking in the other. Jack stopped on the way to his desk as Don Blake emerged from the office.

"What's going on, Don? The President coming through town or something?"

"Nah, not that big," he replied with a half grin. "Big enough to get the Mayor's panties in a twist, though."

"Yeah?" Jack added a laugh. "What's that?"

"Deputy Mayor Reynolds. There's a full-blown investigation under way." Don tilted his head and pushed his face forward. "Man, I don't know *what* he was thinking. Always seemed like an upright kinda guy."

"What the hell did he do?"

"Allegedly," Don emphasized. "We're only investigating at this point."

"Yeah, yeah." Jack's hand motion hurried Don's response.

"He applied for a social security number. No big deal by itself, there could be a number of legitimate reasons. Then, he goes and has someone applying for a driver's license the same day under the same name." Don held up his hand. "Now I know we don't have the most *efficient* system, but damn, ya gotta give us a little respect."

"So what's he doing, creating an identity for someone?"

Don nodded. "Most likely for an illegal domestic. Can you believe that? Throw away your whole damn career to save a few bucks?"

"I'll bet you find that it's more than just a few bucks. But it don't seem worth a career."

Don nodded again. "Guess we don't expect to see that kinda stuff so close to home."

Jack gave a mock punch to Don's shoulder. "Mr. *Mayor* better squeak clean after *this*."

"You damn betcha. I'll let you know what we find out."

Jack continued on to his desk, marveling at the extent people will go to beat the law. He opened a folder lying on the desk and checked the paperwork closely before he signed it. One more cold case solved. It felt good because this time there was no body found, no murder, no tragic accident. A fifteen-year-old boy missing for ten years turned out to be a gay teen running from parents who had handled the situation badly. He was a young man now, who had beaten the odds of prostitution, AIDS, and early death. Jack found him in San Francisco, attending college during the day and tending bar at night.

He closed the file and pushed back his chair. The urge came as expected, especially strong after he closed a case. He gave in as usual and pulled the Panning file from its place in his drawer. He didn't open it, just tapped it repeatedly against the edge of the desk. He had read it so many times that he knew its contents by heart.

There was something extra, though, in the urge today. Something that made him anxious. With his brow knitted tightly, he began tapping the folder against the desk again. Then suddenly, his brow relaxed and he sat straight up in his chair. "That's it!" He froze in his chair, staring straight ahead, almost afraid to believe that he might have it. "That *has* to be it." You've underestimated the resourcefulness of teenagers.

He scrambled to his feet. "Her best friend," he said aloud. "She took her best friend's name." He started to step away from the desk, then stopped. Could it have been that easy? Could she have gotten her social security number, her birth certificate? What was her name?

Quickly he sat back down at his desk, picked up the phone and called upstairs. "Hey, Elaine. Jack Beaman . . . I'm good." He felt the agitation in his voice. "Yep, yep, you sure can. I need you to find me the name of an eleven-year-old girl who was killed riding her bike on Rawlings Road in about 1984, give or take a year on either side. Get me a social security number and you'll be my sweetheart forever." He felt giddy with excitement. "I'll buy you lunch tomorrow."

Two hours later Jack answered the call that he'd been needing for sixteen years. His heart pumped with adrenaline at the sound of Elaine's voice. "Paige Flemming," he repeated. "That's it. Get a number? Great." He wrote the number down and repeated it to her to make absolutely sure he had it right. "This could be the piece that solves a sixteen-year-old puzzle . . . You name the restaurant, sweetheart."

It was too good to be true. Jack stared at the number as if he expected it to disappear as he awakened from a cruel dream. But there it was, in black and white, in his hand. So, put it in the system. What are you waiting for? He stared at the computer screen. You're afraid you're wrong, he chided. You're afraid you've come this close and you're wrong. It's not been wasted energy, you'll find her. If this isn't it, you'll start where this leaves you and go on. You haven't failed as long as you're still kickin'. He took a deep breath and typed the information into the system and waited impatiently through the search.

"Holy Jesus!" he exclaimed. "Yes!" he shouted and jumped from his chair to face the attention of the others in the room. Jack pumped his fist in the air. "There she is. Right there. She's been there all along."

The room erupted into applause and accolades and a smiling

Jack went to work on a trail that started in California and wound its way through twelve different states, to Canada and back, backtracking through states to stop now in Michigan.

His anxiety level was gun-barrel high. "Here I come," he said hoarsely. "Here I come."

Chapter 31

The look on Paige's face told Moni that this wasn't merely a social stop-by. "Is everything okay, Paige?"

"I don't know what I'm doing, Moni."

"Come on, come in the living room."

"Is Katherine here?"

"She's at a meeting, so I'll have to do."

Paige turned in the middle of the room and faced Moni. "No. I mean, that's fine." She turned again, but began to pace rather than sit. "I feel more comfortable talking to you. Is that all right?"

"Of course. Sit, Paige."

She didn't sit, but continued to pace the room.

"Paige, what is it?" Her agitation conjured up the worst possible scenario.

Paige finally stopped, her face contorted into a serious frown, her hands suspended in question at her sides. "What am I doing, Moni?"

Moni took one outstretched hand. "Come here. Sit down and give me a little more to go on, okay?"

She dropped to the couch next to Moni. "I can't leave," she explained. "I know I can't stay, but I can't leave."

Like a crossword puzzle, Moni mused, you have to fill in the spaces. "Marissa."

"What am I going to do?"

"Maybe you should start out by admitting that you're in love with her."

Paige dropped her head into her hands and said nothing.

"It could be time to stay, Paige."

There were long seconds of silence with Paige's head still buried in her hands. Moni placed her hand on Paige's back and moved it gently back and forth.

Paige spoke without moving. "I can't do this to her." She finally raised her head, wiping her eyes quickly with her palms as she did. "But I'm going to—whichever way it goes, I'm going to hurt her."

"Have you told her that you love her?"

Paige shook her head. "Not in words. But it doesn't matter; she'll doubt it anyway when I leave."

"Does she understand why you would have to leave?"

Another shake of her head.

"Tell her, Paige. Give her the choice to go with you."

"What kind of choice is that? What would I be asking her to do, Moni? Leave everything she's built her life around, her friends, her family, and run with me to Canada? Or let me stay in her life right here until I'm caught and then she can visit me in prison once a month?"

"Are you afraid that she might not take either choice?"

Silence again, then, "I'd rather endure that pain than to ruin her life."

"Has she said that she loves you?"

"No, and I don't want her to."

Moni's voice carried an edge of frustration. "Why?" She didn't wait for a response. "God, Paige you've lived most of your life *not* knowing so much. Don't you finally want to know something for sure?"

Paige rested her forehead in her hand and rubbed.

"Find out, Paige. If she loves you, let her decide how much." She took Paige's hand from her face and met her eyes. "You know that I know this from experience—real love will make the sacrifice. You *know* this."

There was something different in Paige's eyes. Moni had noticed it that first day that Paige had come back, but she hadn't been able to identify what it was. Now as she waited for the expected abrupt dismissal and it didn't come, Moni knew what it was—the anger was gone—the gut-tightening, all-consuming, destructive emotion that Moni herself had carried for years. Something else Moni knew from experience was that until you let that anger go there is no room for love.

Moni softened her tone. "You have to let love have its place."

"I want to. I want the feeling I have with her to last for the rest of my life, but . . ."

"But what? You think you're the only one capable of sacrifice? Did your mother ask you to make the sacrifice you made? You chose that sacrifice, didn't you?" A question within a question. "For reasons all your own." She looked for the answer more in her eyes than in her words.

Paige folded her arms tightly over her chest, lifted her face toward the ceiling and closed her eyes. She took a quick breath that flared her nostrils, then she dropped her eyes to Moni's. They had teared despite her attempt to avoid it. Her lip quivered once. "Yes," she whispered, "I chose it."

"Oh, Paige." Moni put her arms around her and held her. "Give Marissa that chance. Whether you stay or go, give her that choice."

The only response Paige offered was a nod against Moni's shoulder.

"Thank you," Moni whispered.

Chapter 32

The sun had dropped behind the buildings in the west, leaving the sky a milky gray. Paige made the usual trip to her room at Miss Emily's for fresh clothes before heading for Marissa's, but this time with a sense of trepidation. Everything Moni had said made perfect sense—as if she could feel what is in my heart. It doesn't matter anymore how she knows these things, it's good enough that she knows. But Moni doesn't have to look into Marissa's eyes and have the conversation that I've promised to have.

Paige waited for traffic, then turned into the modest neighborhood on the north side of the city. She longed for the feeling of comfort she had grown accustomed to lately. She liked the familiar quiet streets here lined with grown maples, watching the season change, and knowing what each day held for her. And she liked being in love—the sense of otherness, of being counted on—she liked feeling worthy of it.

Tonight, though, the conversation with Marissa could change all that. The thought occurred, as she wound slowly through the neighborhood, that she could put it off. The promise was to have the conversation, not *when* to have it. She slowed to a crawl in front of the shake-sided house with the beautiful yard. Bonsai evergreens and lush ferns, and a perennial border that changed color from season to season. It had quickly become her favorite yard.

But yards and familiarity aren't reasons enough to delay the inevitable. Tonight she'd talk with Marissa.

She made the turn onto her street, resolute at least for tonight, when something caught her eye. Something was out of the ordinary. She slowed the car and studied the street. There was never a car parked on the right side of the street, and only the teenager's faded red Grand Prix was usually parked in front of the brick house on the left side. Tonight not one, but two strange cars were parked on her block, one on the right side and one visible around the corner at the other end. Both dark colored, and at least the closest one occupied.

Acid churned her stomach, her heart thudded hard in her chest. She stopped at the stop sign before her block, a complete stop, turn signal on, then made a casual right turn to avoid her own street. Her body began to quiver, not noticeably on the outside, but deep inside. She chanced a quick glance at the side of the nearest car as she made the turn—no markings or stripes or trim, black wall tires with factory hubs—they'd found her.

As slowly as she dared, Paige snaked her way out of the neighborhood, a careful eye on the rearview mirror. She made her way through town, not a mile over the speed limit, stopping at the yellow lights, until she reached the I-94 on-ramp. Seconds later she was headed east toward Detroit and her original destination.

Every mile of highway she drove brought her closer to the familiarity she couldn't escape. The driving, as cautious as she had to be, had calmed her breathing and eliminated the urge to throw up. She was in control of her destiny as long as she could keep moving.

The sign ahead announced the Ambassador Bridge, and suddenly the decision that had troubled her for miles had to be made. Do I try to cross over here, or do I chance two more hours on the road to try crossing at Port Huron? They know I'm in Ann Arbor and the closest border crossing is Detroit. But they don't know that I made them. Can I beat them to it? One mile, I have to decide. Two hours is a long time, it gives them that much longer to notify the border. But they might not think I'd go that far. It's much less traveled. Okay, okay.

Sweat soaked the underarms of her shirt, beaded her forehead, and moistened her palms. She had tried to imagine many times what it would be like, having it come to one decision, one all-important decision, all up to her. But it couldn't be imagined.

The turn toward the bridge loomed ahead. Paige took a deep breath, maintained her speed, and passed it by. For the next 120-plus miles she tucked herself in among the slow traffic in the right lane, no passing, no tailgating. She alternately checked her mirrors and watched for patrols waiting under overpasses and at turnarounds. They were the most tension-filled, anxious miles she had ever driven. The sight of the Blue Water Bridge to Sarnia brought only partial relief. She still had to make it across.

She stopped in line, seven cars back, and watched closely how each car was handled. Each car took about the same amount of time to be cleared through, until the fourth one. A white cargo van was pulled to the side where they opened the back and side doors and searched the inside. The rest of the line moved ahead at a steady pace. One car to go.

Paige pulled the birth certificate and driver's license from her wallet. Left in its place was the small worn social security card she'd kept since she was a little girl. Paige's little red purse, the one part of Paige that couldn't be ripped from her hand on that horrible day so many years ago, had to finally be left behind, but not her identity. What at first was the last tie to her best friend had become a permanent tie for survival.

She tried to breathe normally as she stopped the car next to the booth. She handed the fare to a forty-something, balding man and offered a smile.

"Citizenship?" he asked.

"U.S.," she returned, handing him the birth certificate and driver's license.

"What's your business in Canada?"

"A vacation."

"What are you bringing into the country?"

"Just clothes and toiletries." Her emergency bag tucked always left untouched in her trunk that she had hoped would never become a necessity.

He looked up for the first time and Paige held her breath.

"Enjoy your vacation," he said.

Paige pulled ahead three car lengths before she exhaled fully. Then, unwilling to chance counting her blessings too soon, she drove well into Sarnia and pulled into a parking lot before she stopped and turn off the car. She took a full, deep, chest-expanding breath, laid her head back against the headrest and let it out slowly.

She didn't want to think right now, actually she couldn't think. Her mind was in a state of shock, unable to move beyond the moment. Paige stared vacantly at the visor until her eyes closed and she fell asleep.

Chapter 33

The phone hadn't been out of her hand all morning. Marissa left the chair by the windows and moved for the third time to the couch. She checked her watch again and decided that nine A.M. wasn't too early to call. She hit Evan's number and waited. He picked up on the second ring.

"Hey," she began, trying to keep her voice from breaking, "can you handle rehearsal alone today?"

"Sure. I have to go through two non-dance scenes anyway. What's up?"

"Oh . . ." she stopped when she realized that the control she needed wasn't there. She cleared her throat.

"Mar, what's wrong?"

Her voice had risen to that high, soft place just above tears. "Paige."

"Keep talking to me," he said immediately. "I'm on my way over; tell me what's going on."

She cleared her throat and tried again for control. "She didn't show up last night and . . . she didn't show up at work this morning."

"Don't panic, Mar. It could be nothing to worry about. Maybe she overslept, fell asleep last night or something, you know. It could be that simple."

Her voice dropped into normal range. "But she's not answering her cell phone, either . . . something's wrong, Evan."

"Did you call Moni to see if she's heard from her?"

"It was too late last night to call her."

"Look, if we can't get a hold of Paige by noon, we'll call Moni on her lunch break, okay? Now, I'm going to hang up and try Paige at work for you and I'll be at your place in about ten minutes."

It was less than ten minutes later when Evan let himself in Marissa's front door. She was waiting on the bench in the entranceway, and rose quickly into an embrace.

Tears suddenly spilled down her cheeks. "She's not there, is she?"

"No," he replied. "But maybe there's an explanation."

"I knew," she said, her face buried against his shoulder, "it was a mistake. It's my own fault."

Evan let her cry quietly in his embrace. He kissed the side of her head and tried to reassure her. "Honey, it might be nothing. Give a little more time; let's see what we can find out." He kissed her again. "Okay?"

She made no attempt to leave his arm, to separate herself from his strength and hopefulness. But even that, she feared, would not be able to hold off the inevitable devastation for long.

"Come in here." Evan opened their embrace, took her hand, and led her into the living room. "Let's talk about it."

They settled on the couch where Marissa reached for tissues to dry her tears. "I knew better than to do this, Evan. But she seemed so different than before." She stopped and collected her thoughts. "She's been so thoughtful and sincere. She hasn't missed a day, or a call, or an effort that I expected. This whole time there's been no indication that she might . . ." She dropped her head. "But I knew it was a mistake."

"If this *was* a mistake, honey, we've both made them. It's not the end of the gay world. We'll cry, kick ourselves in our cute little asses, and move on as always."

Encapsulated as only Evan could. But it didn't bring a smile.

"This is a big one," she said, tears beginning to well again. "The biggest mistake."

"The 'L' bomb? That four-letter word that I swore would never pass these lips again?"

The look in her eyes answered for her.

"Yeah," he said, pulling her against him and leaning into the corner of the couch. "How easy it is to forget that that four-letter word gets followed by all the other ones." He kissed the top of her head. "Talk to me about rehearsal. You're coming with me."

Evan was right—he usually was. Calls to Paige's cell phone brought no answers. A call to Moni at noon brought a promise to meet her after work. And the rest of the time, waiting and wondering, would have been intolerable. So she went to rehearsal with him. Although she wasn't able to totally concentrate on lines and vocal inflections and projection, she also wasn't able to completely disengage. Every time she made another unanswered phone call or drifted into anxiety and self-pity, her attention was snapped back by a blooper or a question, or Evan plopping himself down in the seat next to her with a comment that could not be repeated out loud.

Now, she waited for Moni and whatever relief *she* could offer. Like many things in her life now, waiting for help from someone else was not what she had envisioned herself doing. But since the accident, waiting on help and support of others had become an integral, and still uncomfortable, part of her life. Except where Paige was concerned.

What she needed from Paige she had never needed from anyone else. It had been more than encouragement; she had plenty of that from friends and family. Paige had challenged her—brazenly, irreverently, and honestly. And it had been more than caring, or even love, that she needed from her; that, too, was available elsewhere. She needed Paige to show her that she was desirable, intimately desirable. And Paige had done that, better than expected. So well, in fact, that there had been no thoughts of how long it would last, or if either of them wanted it to.

Each day had been filled with new challenges, sharing each other's successes, wanting to be at their best for each other. The

169

nights had held their own excitement, new lovers discovering how to please each other and the confidence that comes with doing that well. More surprising, though, than the way Paige left, was the realization of how much she did not want their time together to end.

Moni breezed in, made her apologies for being late, and got right to the subject. "Have you talked with Paige yet?"

"No," Marissa replied. "I don't know what to think."

"It's had me thinking and so distracted today that I forgot to take roll in two of my classes."

Marissa's tone was apologetic. "I should have waited and called you after work."

"No, it's fine. I needed the time to decide some things."

"Paige talked with you, didn't she?"

Moni answered with a nod. "I've always considered anything she tells me to be said in confidence. I didn't even share them with Katherine until I had permission."

Marissa's hope for an answer, held like an inflated balloon, began to lose air. There *was* an explanation, but she wasn't going to hear it.

"Tell me something," Moni began. "Are you in love with Paige? Push past hurt and the verge of anger and confusion, and tell me if you've been able to say the words?"

"Not until now," she admitted, but she held Moni's eyes directly. "I am hopelessly in love with her."

Moni hesitated, dropped her gaze and leaned forward to rest her forearms on her thighs. She sat there that way, obviously still undecided, until, "She's in love with you, too."

Marissa let go of an audible breath and dropped her head to her hands. She wouldn't cry. The relief she felt was laden with questions and uncertainty. It showed on her face as she lifted her head. "Then what the hell is going on?"

"I can't watch you like this," Moni said. "I don't know for sure why she left, and I certainly don't know why she didn't talk with you as she promised me she would, but you deserve to know what I think."

"I've put you in a bad situation; I realize that, but—"

"I put myself there. I only hope that what I tell you helps rather than hurts the situation."

Whatever information Moni had wasn't immediately forthcoming. What was she deciding—how much to tell, where to start? Could it be that bad? Who have I fallen in love with? She's not a career criminal or a murderer—is she? "If you knew that you would find a truth/That brings a pain that can't be soothed/Would you change?" The words, like the rest of the Tracy Chapman song, had filtered through her thoughts for weeks. She must have listened to it a hundred times, sung the words and listened to their deeper messages. She was sure that they would give her the insight into Paige that she had begun to crave. But now, do I want to know?

"I'm going to tell you what I'm pretty sure of, and then what I *think. That's* the best I can do."

"Please, just tell me, Moni."

"Paige grew up with an alcoholic mother and an abusive stepfather. When she was sixteen she watched her mother stab her stepfather to death."

Marissa frowned. Just a bit more disturbing than I knew.

Moni continued. "Paige told me that she had to pry the knife from her mother's hand to stop her from stabbing him. In the struggle she thought that her stepfather was getting up from the chair. It scared her so badly that she ran to the barn and hid. That's where the police found her. They found the knife in the field where she threw it."

A *lot* more disturbing. She was starting to get the picture.

"The rest of the story is pretty sketchy. They were going to prosecute her as an adult for his murder. I'm not sure how, but she got free and has been running ever since."

Stunned, Marissa moved her head very slowly from side to side. "All those years? What kind of a life is that?"

"Among other things," Moni replied, "quite a stressful one."

"But, if her mother did it, and she was a battered woman . . ."

"The statistics are staggering, and Paige knows them by heart, of women imprisoned for life for killing an abusive husband or boyfriend. The battered-woman defense didn't have much of a track record back then. If *Paige's* case had been successfully defended, then—"

"Her mother most likely would have gone to prison."

"Yes, and you can understand her choice when you realize that she trusts the law of percentages more than she does the police—her stepfather was a cop. If it had been any other abusive son-of-a-bitch maybe they could have gotten help."

Marissa slumped against the back of the couch. "So I can nix the thought that they may have given up looking for her?"

"Paige certainly has nixed the idea. Katherine and I have tried to talk to her about getting legal help. Either of them would have a better chance now."

"But she's too scared."

"It's all she's ever known. Put yourself in her place."

"Yes," Marissa agreed. "I'd be scared too."

Moni dropped forward again on her forearms, obviously thinking, staring at the rug. Finally, she asked, "You didn't ask me if I believe her, that her mother was the one who killed him."

Marissa's eyes came slowly to Moni's. "Why would I question that?"

Moni shrugged slightly. "Would you question whether a bond for a negligent, alcoholic mother is strong enough to cause you to spend the rest of your life running?"

The look in Paige's eyes when she spoke of her mother was dulled in Marissa's memory. The love Paige had seen in her mother's eyes had clearly shone in her own. "No," Marissa said. "I would not question it."

Moni nodded and smiled. "I don't know why, but my heart doesn't question it either."

"And Paige was supposed to tell me all of this?"

"I made her promise to take the risk of letting you know how she feels, to find out how you feel about her. She was going to lay it all out there and let you decide what was best for you."

"Whether or not I loved her enough to go with her?"

"Bottom line."

"Do you know where she is?"

"Now we're in that 'what I think' area. She was on her way to Canada when she stopped here. My best guess is that something spooked her and that's where she is."

Would I have gone with her? Leave what I know for something I'm not sure of? What would I have told her? "And now I'm left to question how much love it would have taken for me to leave, and how much it would have taken for her to stay."

Moni was silent, looking blankly at the table in front of her.

"And what," Marissa continued, "would make her leave without even a phone call."

"I think something spooked her. And whatever it was may not even seem logical to us."

"And you know this how?"

"I've seen it, more than once." Moni replied. "I'll give one good example. Years ago we played on a softball team together. We had this cute little black girl playing third and during this one game a group of black guys that we didn't know kept hanging around close to the baseline and bothering her. The umpires asked them to leave, but they didn't. So a bunch of our guys from the stands armed themselves with bats and that's when someone called the police. The city had been having race problems so it wasn't unusual to see more than one cop car roll up. Both teams had retreated to the dugouts and I was standing next to Paige when she suddenly just bolted. In a matter of seconds she had climbed the fence at the back of the dugout and took off at a full sprint into a nearby neighborhood. It wasn't logical. She left her car and everything. We looked for her for hours but couldn't find her. She showed up at the coach's house two days later . . . I just learned to accept it because it was Paige."

"Her fear is that real."

"Yeah," Moni replied, her stare locked on the newspaper facing her on the table.

Moments later she grabbed the paper for a closer look. "Hey, this is Paige's street," she said, moving quickly to sit beside Marissa on the couch. "Look."

They studied the picture together—a handcuffed man being

escorted to an unmarked police car. The article described a successful stake-out and bust just two doors down from where Paige rented a room.

"They busted them at two in the morning," Moni noted. "What if Paige saw the cops and thought they were waiting for her?"

"In unmarked cars?"

"It's possible. She's very alert, very suspicious . . . Oh, yeah," Moni concluded.

"You really think so?"

Moni nodded. "She's running scared.

"What can we do?" Marissa asked, eyes wide and anxious. "We have to let her know. I don't want her scared like that."

"Just leave another message on her cell phone, hope she hasn't tossed it—and wait.

Chapter 34

A chilling rain distorted the glow from the streetlights into Van Gogh–like orbs and beat steadily upon Paige's head and shoulders. Her hair hung in ringlets about her face, her shirt clung tightly to her skin and bra. She had forgotten her jacket.

Hands in the dampening pockets of her jeans, Paige crossed the street and returned to the motel. The neighborhood bar down the street had lost its appeal as soon as the man in the green plaid shirt introduced himself. Maybe tomorrow she would find a gay bar, or be lucky enough to find a women's bar—a place to find company to chase away the loneliness and forget the fears, for a little while. Tonight, though, was ending like the last five, alone in a motel room.

She fished the key from her pocket and let herself in. The air was musky with the smell of old carpet and stale cigarette smoke, but she had stayed in worse. The bathroom was sadly outdated but clean, and the bed was sleepable.

Although she had experienced the physicality of it many times before, this time the experience was different. Fears swarmed in the night, overwhelming her and leaving her defenseless against them. She struggled to quell them, turning on the lights and the TV and leaving them on until daylight. But the pacing didn't stop until alcohol sat her down and sleep didn't come until she passed out. It was the only anesthesia she had.

Paige finished toweling herself down and donned the dry clothes that she had washed out yesterday. She fixed another drink and braced herself for the onslaught of loneliness the likes of which she had not experienced since Derrick died.

The overhead light was a harsh reminder that tonight even the alcohol couldn't save her from her most torturous memory. There was nothing to protect her from the vision of his gaunt face and dying eyes, or to save her from the feel of his hand slipping from hers, or to shut out the high-pitched sound of the end of his life. Nothing protected her from the razor-sharp realization that she was totally alone for the first time in her life.

Like now, she had felt the deepest pain of it at night. Not the first night after his death, or the second, she had been too numb. But the third night, the desire to see the light dance again in his eyes, and to hear the soothing sound of his laughter, brought the tears. The tears turned to sobs that echoed in the emptiness.

Over the years since then, she'd become accustomed to the loneliness. She learned to temper it with distractions—a job, the challenge of a new locale, the company of a woman. But nothing had completely taken it away, until Marissa.

She hadn't noticed exactly when the self-imposed restrictions began dropping away. She'd made no conscious decision to care so deeply, or to arrange each day and night around her. She didn't purposely challenge fate by waking each morning in Marissa's bed or letting love wrap her instincts in cotton candy. One day the restrictions were safely in place, the next thing she knew they were gone. In their place was a love and happiness she never thought she'd experience.

Paige placed the empty glass on the bedside table and leaned back against the headboard. The tears began, and with nothing to stop them, they would soon echo an emptiness to rival Derrick's death. What have I done? She covered her eyes with her hand. Why couldn't I stop? Why couldn't I just stop?

Crying offered no relief from the pain—it hadn't then and she knew it wouldn't now. But she couldn't stop. She had no more control over the tears than she did over what caused them. She would have to grieve for Marissa as she had for Derrick. This time, though, she wasn't sure she could make it through.

Paige opened her eyes. The room had stopped moving, but she was still sick. Beyond the nausea and the shaking, her heart was sick. Infant that it was, her heart continued crying its own tears even after the physical ones had dried. Untouched by the effects of a week of alcohol, it beat out its pain like a frightened child, and made her question whether prison could be any worse a hell. She looked reality in the face and realized that there would be no soothing whispers, no comforting embrace or gentle lips against her brow. There would be no help now for her pain short of Marissa's voice.

Suddenly there was nothing as important, nothing she wouldn't sacrifice. Paige picked up the phone. She closed her eyes and waited for Marissa to answer.

The sound, when she answered, was the calm Paige needed. "I needed to hear your voice."

"Paige! God, baby, where are you?"

"I'm in Canada. I want to explain."

"I already know, Paige. Moni told me. I know you're afraid, but it's all right."

"I am. I am afraid. But I'm more afraid of never seeing you again."

Marissa tried again. "It's okay—"

"No, Marissa, it's not okay. My life's not okay. It's not okay to love you, or for you to love me."

"But I do."

The words themselves didn't surprise her, neither did the concept of Marissa loving her, but something stopped her thought process in its tracks. She had no plan of action past this point, only fantasies, only words spoken to make-believe lovers and hopes for a make-believe future.

"I love you, Paige," said Marissa, her voice clearly beginning to be affected by emotion. "Enough to go wherever I need to go to be with you."

Snapped into the realization of what she was hearing, Paige replied, "I can't ask that of you."

"You don't have to. It's time somebody finally risks something for you."

"Is there anything that I can say that would change your mind?"

"I've actually thought about that, and there is something," Marissa replied. "You can tell me that you don't love me."

"Then there's nothing I can say."

"Do you know that I'm smiling?" Marissa asked.

"Yes, I know." Paige stopped before the mirror above the desk. "And I know what happiness looks like."

"I'll look a lot better when I can see you."

"That's part of what I wanted to explain," Paige began. "I couldn't take any chances. Undercover cops were waiting on my street."

"But not for you. That's what I wanted to tell you. It was a drug bust on your block."

The relief registered immediately. Stress shot audibly from Paige's lungs as she dropped to sit on the bed. "Are you sure?"

"We saw the article and picture in the newspaper. I saved it so that you can see for yourself. It wasn't you."

Paige lay back on the bed and stared at the ceiling. She wanted her mind to feel the same relief that her body felt, but it didn't.

"I can't imagine what you must have just gone through, honey. What can I do? Can I come there?"

"No," Paige replied softly. "You can't comfortably travel that far yet."

"Even with a whole pain pill?"

Paige smiled at the gesture. "I'll be there tomorrow."

"Are *you* sure?"

"If I wait too long, I'm worried that I'll wake up and realize this conversation was just part of a dream."

Chapter 35

The police station was the last place Geri Panning wanted to visit. And she wouldn't have, had she been able to ignore the awful feeling that had been nagging her for the past two days.

Jack not showing up at the diner for lunch and not bothering to leave a message on her answering machine wasn't normal. Nor was the fact that he wasn't answering his cell phone.

She'd been stood up before, more times than she cared to remember. And she'd been *dumped*, too. But she had been so sure that Jack Beaman was a different breed of man. It had been easy to rationalize away the thought that having someone like Jack interested in her was too good to be true, because of how good it made her feel. Is that vanity, to want to claim the attention of a man of his caliber? How many smart, accomplished men have come knocking? And what makes me think I deserve one that does? Whatever it is, it's strong enough to get me down *here* today.

The officer at the desk in the front had directed her down the hall to the large room. She had expected it to have changed more over the years, but it seemed only the faces were different. The first detective she asked pointed her to a desk near the center of the room.

As she approached the empty desk, a detective in tie and shirt-sleeves at the adjoining desk asked, "Ma'am, how can I help you?"

"I'm looking for Jack Beaman."

He smiled and added a chuckle. "That's a twist. O' JB's the one usually doing the looking. I'm sorry," he said, standing and extending his hand. "He's on the road with a hot lead on a very cold murder case. Maybe I can help you."

"Oh, no," she said with a weak smile. "I really need to talk with Jack."

"Well, he's gonna be a happy man if he comes home with this one. Can I tell him to give you a call when he gets back in?"

"No, that's . . . I'll try his cell."

The desire to run from the building as fast as she could was barely controlled. Geri's legs shook with the possibility that what she had prayed to God would never happen was happening.

"Please, no," she pleaded as her shaking hand made opening the car door difficult. "Not my Annie, God. Not my Annie." She sat with a tight grip on the steering wheel until the shaking stopped long enough to drive home. She had to get home. No stops. No stops. Just get home.

Her first call was to her sponsor, who in turn encouraged her second call.

"Jackie, this is Geri Panning. I'm sorry to bother you."

"It's no bother. Is there something wrong?"

"Please be honest with me," Geri's voice shook uncontrollably. "I need you to be."

Jackie's voice carried a maternal calm. "What is it, Geri?"

"You have to tell me where Jack is."

"Geri I—I don't know."

It took a conscious effort to calm her voice and lower her tone to below desperation level. "No, please," Geri tried again. "You don't understand. I have to know where he is. It's important."

"I only know that he's away on a case. I don't know where, Geri. That is the truth."

Her voice rose with anxiety. "It's my Annie, isn't it? I know it's Annie. What have I done?"

As she was speaking, Jewelle Roberts let herself in the side door, poured two cups of coffee, and placed one before Geri at the kitchen table.

"It could be," Jackie replied "I won't lie to you. It's been a personal challenge, and for him to be gone for days like this—well, it could be."

Geri reached across the table to grasp the dark thick hand of the woman who had been her rock for seven years, and continued speaking into the phone. "I have to talk to him, Jackie. He'll answer your call, please call him for me. Ask him to talk to me?"

"It's yes?" Jewelle asked as Geri hung up.

Geri squeezed her hand and nodded.

Jewelle covered both Geri's hands with her own, closed her eyes and whispered a prayer. "Now," she said with the slow, deliberate cadence that Geri had come to rely on. "We've got *all* we need to deal with this."

"It's too late. Don't you see what I've done?"

"Whoa, now, where ya goin' with this?"

"It was my own selfishness, wanting his attention like that. I haven't changed at all. I'm the same self-centered woman who satisfied her own needs over her babies'." She stood up from the table and turned to face the door. A shaky hand pushed errant strands of hair from her forehead, only to have them fall again. "Look what I've done, Jewelle. I've done it again."

"Hold on, honey. Come on now, keep talking to Jewelle."

Obediently, Geri returned to her seat at the table, but perched herself on the edge of the chair as if a school bell would send her racing for the door.

"Let's not go to the 'needin' and the wantin'," Jewelle began, "'cause the Lord knows we all need things we don't want and want things we don't need. That ain't the crime—the crime's in the denyin'. Now, let's get to *right* now—today." She clasped her hand over Geri's forearm as it rested on the table. "We don't know that it's Annie he's after until we talk to Jack."

"*I* know," she replied, tapping her fist over her heart. "I've always known in here he hadn't given up. And I let him get to her." Her voice began to rise. "I let him, Jewelle, because I wanted him to be someone he's not." She was almost shouting now. "It was all about me, and he knew it would be. He played me *so* good. What kind of man is that?" She dropped her head and the tone of her voice. "Only a selfish, stupid woman would let this happen."

"You didn't let anything happen. Look at me, Geri." She waited and Geri raised her head. "Wanting to be happy is not selfish, it's human. Now let's talk this through. What could you have done that would've helped him find her?"

"I've been trying to figure it out. What was it I said? Was there something I knew all along?" She looked pleadingly into the eyes she knew held no judgment. "I never would have said anything, not if I knew what I was sayin'—never. Even if that were the only way I'd ever see her again."

"Speculating's gonna get us nowhere, honey." She patted Geri's forearm. "You gotta make that call. Let's see if he'll talk to you."

Geri nodded and picked up the phone immediately. Her hand still shook as she punched in the number, and her eyes returned to Jewelle's as she waited. A moment later she dropped her gaze and laid the phone back on the table.

"That's okay. Leave a message, and we'll keep trying."

"His voice mail is full."

"Then I guess we're gonna need a fresh pot of coffee."

Coffee and Jewelle for the long night Geri knew was ahead. It would be filled with anxiety and self-loathing, and the kind of emotional discomfort that alcohol and drugs had for years kept her from feeling. But not tonight. She'd have to feel the feelings and deal with the doubt, and live through the uncertainty.

Jewelle will help get me through this, however long it takes, but there is nothing she can do to help Annie. Annie is my responsibility, she always has been. My responsibility and my failure.

Her body relaxed as her mind settled into resolve. For once in my life Annie is going to come first. Whatever it takes, I won't fail her again. I'll protect her this time and she'll know how much I love her. This time I know how to do it.

Chapter 36

Paige sat in line at the border, her thoughts vastly different than a week ago. Fear of her life changing forever in the worst possible way had been replaced with thoughts of a wonderful change. Thoughts of where to live were very different now, tinged with excitement and, for the first time, consideration of a lover's needs.

Without question, we'll come back to live in Canada, but not here. Marissa needs to be near a bigger city, lots of cultural organizations, the arts, a university. I'll get some training this time for a good job, something that will let us save some money for a house. We'll find one that we can make another dance room in, and a little weight room so we can continue her therapy at home.

The anxiousness she felt was coupled now with an excitement that hadn't been possible before Marissa. At last it was possible to cultivate it and enjoy it, because now there was a plan for the future and someone to share it with. In all her fantasies and daydreams, she had imagined that it would feel this good.

The line moved along at a steady pace. With one car in front of her, Paige sang along with the *Dirty Dancing* soundtrack. She knew every piece by heart now, and could visualize the choreography to each one. She had never been more proud of anything she'd done, and now she would even get to see the end result. The show's in two weeks. I can take the chance of waiting two weeks. Then, after the show, we'll leave to start our life together like any normal couple.

She readied her identification and money, and pulled up next to the booth. A man with a ruddy complexion compared her with the picture on her license, then looked past her to ask, "Anyone else in the car?"

"No."

He kept her license and looked through a list of names.

The events of 9/11 and the resulting list of questionable names made it tougher to come into the country than it did to leave it. This much she expected. The name Flemming shouldn't raise any red flags. But what happened next was not expected.

"Ma'am," he said, handing her back her identification. "I need you to pull the car right over there where the security officers are standing."

It felt as though something with the weight of a bowling ball dropped through her mid-section. Her chest tightened as if a band were keeping her from taking a deep breath. She didn't remember consciously moving the car or what was said or how she came to stand next to one of the officers. She watched numbly as her car was methodically searched. One thought ran a repeated loop through her mind—an attempt at reassurance: she was a random selection, just like at the airports, it means nothing.

Many minutes passed before the loop slowed long enough for conscious thought to form. What was it she had just heard on the news? Was it methamphetamine? It was one of the big drugs, and Canada was the largest source of it coming into the US. Okay, times have changed since the last time I came back across. No drugs, and I'm not a terrorist. There's nothing to worry about. Smile. Be polite. Another car had been pulled over earlier and they were fine.

"It's going to be a little while longer," the officer next to her explained. "You can go ahead and fold your clothes back up and put 'em back in your bag."

Finally, something that sounded encouraging. She began

folding and repacking while every cavity of her car was examined. Focusing on her task helped relieve a portion of the anxiety. It shouldn't be much longer. *I need to call Marissa as soon as I'm back on the road.* She checked her watch. *I'll be at least an hour late.* She zipped her bag closed and finally took a deep breath.

"Paige Flemming?" a voice asked from behind her.

She turned as a sixty-something man in a suit and tie grasped her wrist. Something jump-started her adrenaline, and suddenly the gravity of what was happening hit her before the words did.

"Or better known in North Branch as Ann Panning. I'm sure you don't remember *me*," he said, "but I've never forgotten you."

It's over.

"You're under arrest," he stated as he clicked the handcuffs in place, "for the murder of Randall Buschell."

Then came the rights that she had heard so many times in her nightmares. But before he had finished saying them, the acid boiling in her gut exploded violently. Vomit spewed from Paige's mouth, splattering over the officer's pant leg and steaming on contact with the pavement.

"Goddamn," the officer swore, as Paige bent at the waist, emptying what little was left in her stomach.

"I'm sorry," she muttered, unable to wipe her mouth.

Her legs started to buckle, and Jack hooked his hand under a handcuffed arm and pulled Paige up.

She coughed and spit in an attempt to clear the bitter taste from her mouth and throat. Her voice was shaky. "I need to clean up."

Jack tugged hard on her arm and turned her toward him. "Not a chance," he replied gruffly. "I was there when it worked for you the first time." He directed his explanation to the security officers. "She was sixteen and nobody thought she could squeeze through a second-story bathroom and shimmy down a down-spout." His eyes returned to Paige. "But there's no way you're going to embarrass *this* detective. Come on," he said, pulling her toward his car. "We've got a drive ahead of us."

❖ ❖ ❖

185

The cuffs that were pressed uncomfortably between her back and the back of the seat cut into her wrists, but Paige didn't notice. She stared stoically through the car window where the symbols of so much of her life seemed to pass without consequence for possibly the last time. Her mind had retreated to the place of safety it had found long ago. During the scary times she'd go there—to the smallest place she could find, and wrap herself in something that she could control. It wasn't much; at first a wooden box in the barn where her stepfather's shouts and her mother's screams could no longer be heard. Then, later, to the make-believe family and house that she had created in her mind. Now, to her secret memory world, full of truths that had been hers and that no one could take away.

"We're going to drive straight through," Jack said, peering into the rearview mirror. "You'll eat and use the restroom when we stop for gas."

Paige made no acknowledgment that she had heard him. She was too far away in a world where she and Marissa lived.

They traveled for hours without so much as a word passing between them. The stop for gas was accompanied by only the necessary directives. The handcuffs came off only while Paige used the bathroom, and Jack waited outside the stall. They were locked in front only long enough for her to eat.

She had no thought as to eating or not eating, but the first few bites of the sandwich made it clear that she should not. Paige closed the cardboard container over what was left and set it on the seat next to her. She sipped her bottle of water until Jack finished eating.

"You made me angry," Jack said, turning in the front seat, "for a lot of years." He stared into Paige's expressionless face. "A teenager outsmarting North Branch's finest. I'll tell you it was a full-out effort. Randall Buschell was a good cop."

Paige abruptly turned her face to the window. What does that say if someone like Buschell, with no apparent human qualities, can be a good cop?

"But the longer you were out there," he continued, "the more determined I became. And the more I believed the sign we have

186

in the cold-case unit: 'The better the adversary, the more commendable the capture.'"

I made you look good in the long run.

"Hat's off to you—kudos to me."

"Yeah," Paige replied, maintaining her stare out the window. "I get it."

"I do feel bad about your mother, though."

Paige turned quickly to meet his eyes.

"She's a good woman. And for what it's worth, she really loves you."

"*You*," she said, fiercely fighting immediate anger and unwelcome tears, "have no right to tell me that." She clenched her jaw and turned back to the window.

"Yeah? Maybe not. But I did." He wiped his mustache with a napkin. "Thought you should know.

He left the front, opened the back door and motioned Paige out. He re-secured the cuffs behind her back and ducked her back into the car.

On through Indiana they drove in silence. She'd seen him periodically eyeing her in the rearview mirror. Gloating. Counting his kudos. Hearing the cheers they'd give him when he walked in the station with her. Sometimes she stared back at him, forcing him to change his focus to the highway. She wanted to ask him how, but it would only allow him to gloat out loud. He'd tell her sooner or later anyway, he wouldn't be able to resist.

At this point, how didn't matter anyway—it was over. If she'd followed her instincts, he may never have found her. She had only herself to blame. The question she would someday have to answer for herself was whether love had been worth the risk. Right now, with the taste of love so fresh, the answer was easy. But she had only just begun to feel the consequences.

They were close to the Illinois border when Jack's phone rang. He checked it as he had the other times, but this time he answered it.

"Rachael, is everything okay?" As he listened, he checked the right lane and quickly switched lanes. "What happened?"

He had barely slowed enough to take the unplanned exit, but

was able to bring the car to a sudden stop at the end of the curve. "Oh, Jesus! How is she?" He shoved the gear in park and listened. "No, no. I'm just coming into Illinois . . . I will, sweetie, I will, as fast as I can get there. You call me the minute she gets out of surgery." He kept rubbing his hand across his forehead as he spoke. "Was Bradley hurt?" Jack took a deep breath and closed his eyes as he let it out. "Okay, okay. Did he see it happen? Goddamn . . . It was Dan, wasn't it?" He nodded as he spoke, "I knew this would happen. I *knew* it. Do they have him? . . . All right, I'm getting back on the road. Rachael, you call me . . . It's gonna be all right. I'll be there soon."

Jack was on the phone again almost immediately as he pulled the car across the overpass to the ramp. "Bill. I know about Jackie. I need you on it. His name is Dan Campbell. You need to find him, Bill. What I mean is you need to find him before I do, because I swear to God if I get my hands on that son-of-a-bitch . . . I'm counting on that. Thanks, Bill."

The car entered the highway and Jack punched the speed up past the limit. Paige could barely hear him talking, to himself. She couldn't tell what he was saying, but the phone conversations had told her all she needed to draw her own conclusions. But by the grace of God, Detective. By the grace of God.

He held the speed well over the legal limit, passing slower traffic as if it would actually get him to the hospital by the time his daughter came out of surgery. Paige could feel his desperation, she knew desperation. And his anger. He was righteously angry, a state of mind, a state of heart that would destroy him regardless of how justified it was. She could tell him that, but he wouldn't be able to listen.

She watched him, his hand tight on the wheel, his focus strictly bent on his mission and she felt sorry for him. *His* turmoil had just begun. She hoped his journey would be shorter than her own.

The phone rang again and Jack grabbed it immediately. "Sweetie, tell me she's going to be all right . . . Oh, God, thank you . . . but she's going to be okay." He had changed lanes and slowed the car considerably. "Make sure she knows that Bradley's okay . . . Tell her that I love her . . . I know, sweetie. I'll see you soon."

It was two miles to the next exit. Jack pulled off there and stopped the car in the lot of the first gas station he came to. He leaned back against the headrest and covered his eyes with his hand.

During the next few moments Paige tried to decide what to say, or if to say anything at all. He had cut her no breaks—her wrists were bruised, her back and shoulders were stiff and sore from hours of riding with her hands behind her back. But he was clearly crying.

Finally, Paige offered, "I'm glad your daughter is going to be okay."

He nodded as he sat upright and wiped his eyes. "She'll have to have more surgery when she's stronger."

"I'm sorry."

He met her eyes in the rearview mirror. "This never should have happened. I could've stopped it."

"How would you have done that?"

Jack turned to face her. "I'd have made sure that he never came near her."

"Twenty-four-seven? Why was she with him?"

He clenched his teeth and spat his answer. "She loved the son-of-a-bitch."

"And you could've stopped them? A whole police force couldn't keep a *cop* from nearly killing my mother. What makes you so special?"

For a moment she couldn't tell where the anger was going. Out of instinct, she readied herself for whatever defense was possible. But it wasn't necessary. He channeled it—right where she had channeled hers.

"Why?" he shouted. "Why *him*?"

The question, Paige knew, wasn't directed at her. He didn't expect an answer, because he knew there wasn't one. He needed to vent and that, too, she understood.

So he vented. "She put herself at risk; she put her child at risk. For what? And what kind of an animal beats a woman?"

"Or a child?" she added. "He would be next."

Teeth clenched tightly, he replied, "I swear to God I'd kill him."

She looked Jack directly in the eyes and took the chance. "But by the grace of God?"

He turned sharply away and started the car. Without further discussion he moved the car next to a pump. Paige waited while he filled the tank and moved again, closer to the door of the station. This time when he escorted her into the building he removed the handcuff from one hand and attached it to his own wrist. Much less obvious, much less embarrassing for Paige. He checked the bathroom for windows, and for the first time he released her and waited outside in the hallway. Small gestures in themselves, but combined with leaving her hands cuffed in front after they ate, they seemed to Paige to be a statement.

Once more on the road, Paige watched the mirror for Jack's eyes. Minutes later she met them there. "Thank you," she said.

He nodded and refocused on the road ahead.

Jack's voice woke her from much-needed sleep. Paige raised her head slowly, rubbing the stiff ache in her neck with one hand-cuffed hand. "I'm sorry, what did you say?"

"We'll be there in about an hour," he repeated. "There are some things that I want to tell you before we get there, and some other things I'd like to know."

His eyes seemed to ask permission in the mirror. Paige nodded in return.

"I haven't told your mother that I found you. I couldn't face her. She knows in her heart, she left all these messages on my voice mail pleading with me." He stopped and cleared his throat. "She blames herself for letting you down again. What I want you to know is that I found you on my own; she had nothing to do with it. I did this because it's my job, and I know she will hate me for it for the rest of her life. And I want you to know that your mother is a decent, loving woman."

"And how do you know this?"

"I went to school with her. And I have gotten to know her again over the last year."

"For the purpose of getting to me."

A long silence ensued before Jack replied, "At first."

"How is she?"

"Clean and sober for seven years."

There it is, in so few words. Does he know that it's all he has to say? Paige lay her head back against the seat as tears formed and rolled gently down her face. It was the only question that needed answering in all this time, the only one that held justification, the one that said all was not in vain. Her chest lifted in a breath light and full and free—the breath of a child exhausted after play.

She opened her eyes to Jack's voice and wiped her face on the upper sleeve of her shirt.

"The things I'd like to know aren't directly related to your case," he said. "But you still don't have to answer them if you'd rather not. Remember you don't have to talk to me at all until you have proper counsel."

"I know."

He gave her a few more seconds before he asked, "I assume that you know your mother was an alcoholic."

"And my stepfather."

"Did they try to get help?"

"My mother did, a couple of times when I was old enough to know what it meant—the meetings and *those* fights."

"She couldn't get your stepfather to go with her?"

"No. The second time she tried, she had to hide it from him."

"I suppose it would have been hard *not* to drink, if he was drinking."

Paige's tone gained a hard edge. "I watched him grab her by the hair and pour straight whiskey down her throat. He kept shouting in her face that she thought she was too good to drink with him. He called her names no one deserves to be called."

"But she stayed."

"She stayed alive."

"She never filed a report against him."

"Sure she did. He brought it home and tore it up in front of her. Then told her every place she'd been during the last week,

191

everyone she'd talked to. For an eight-year-old it was a confusion in hatred."

"As much as I'd love it, I have to advise you not to incriminate yourself."

"I'm not talking about my stepfather."

"Your mother?" he asked.

Paige stared for a few moments at the growing familiarity of the landscape. "I hated her," she said, "and for as long as I can remember, I've hated that I love her."

Paige endured the processing, the further dehumanization of pictures and finger-printing, and was finally allowed her call for help. One that should have been made years ago.

"Moni—"

"God, Paige," Moni replied. "Where the hell are you? Poor Marissa is a basket case."

I'm in North Branch, Moni. I was arrested at the border. I'm going to need that attorney."

"I'm on it right now, *and* on the next plane there."

Chapter 37

The metallic smell of the hospital brought haunting visions as Jack walked briskly down the hallway to Jackie's room. But even the visions of his cancer-ridden wife, pale and weak, did not prepare him for what he saw when he entered the room.

His gut tightened in a sickening knot. He fought consciously to keep his breath under control, to keep from shouting out his hurt and anger. This wasn't the result of a car accident, or disease, this was purposeful and twisted, and this was his baby—his flesh and blood.

He took her hand and tried to look past the swelling and bruises and dried blood defining the cuts to see the eyes that had always held so much hope. The instant they opened to his touch, he vowed, "No one will ever hurt you again. I swear to God, baby," he whispered.

"Daddy," she replied through lips barely able to move. Her eyes closed again, squeezing tears from their corners.

"Oh, shh." He offered gentle utterances as he carefully wiped the tears away.

"I'm sorry," she whispered.

"It *was* Dan, wasn't it?"

She tried to lick her lips and Jack quickly wet the little sponge on a stick and rubbed it over them for her. "Please, Daddy, don't hurt him."

"You look hard into my eyes," he said, "and you'll know that I'll never make that promise."

Her voice was weak, and muffled by the thickness of her swollen lips. "It was my fault."

"No," he said firmly. His nostrils flared with barely controlled emotion. "It was not your fault. *No* man ever has the right to put his hands on you, or to disrespect you in any way. You did *not* cause him to do this. And he will know that, if it's the very last thing I do on this earth."

She made one last attempt. "He needs help, Daddy. I knew he needed help."

"Accepting help was *his* responsibility. You could not control that." He touched her head gently with his fingers. "You just loved the wrong man."

"She's been waiting out there for hours, Jack."

Jack thanked his partner with a hand to his shoulder and headed for the conversation that he could no longer avoid.

Geri Panning sat alone on the bench near the station entrance. Her head was bent forward, her hands clasped together in her lap. Jack approached the bench and took her hands in his own as he sat beside her.

She locked onto his eyes and said only, "Why?"

The question was one that had begun to bother him somewhere in Illinois.

"Partly because it's my job, and it was the right thing to do," he began. "Partly because," he paused and looked into the busy workings of his station. "I wanted to be able to be the one to right a professional embarrassment." He returned to face Geri. "And partly out of ignorance."

"I trusted you," she said. "Like a foolish old woman I wanted to believe that you really wanted to spend time with me."

"But I—"

"I don't blame you. I can't say that you ever lied to me, maybe let me believe what I wanted. I accept that responsibility." She broke their contact and stood. "Now I want to see my Annie."

Jack stood and took her by the elbow. "She's not like I expected her to be," he said, guiding her down the hall. "I sort of expected a grown-up version of a street kid. You know, rough and tough." Not really what I meant to say. This is not going well at all. "She has your eyes, you know. I knew who she was as soon as I looked in her eyes." Still no response from Geri.

Jack seated her in a room and called for Ann to be escorted up from the holding cell. He waited in the adjoining room, watching through the two-way glass. Geri looked dazed to him, as if she were struggling to handle something she wasn't prepared for.

What have I done to her? So hell-bent on a mission, succeed at all cost. I couldn't see that Geri was part of that cost. I couldn't see how much I cared. Now it's too late.

Was I that arrogant that I actually thought that she would forgive me? Did I think we'd just pick up where we left off—never mind that I put your daughter in prison? I *wasn't* thinking. I had no idea that it would matter this much.

Geri sat straighter in her chair as the woman that her little girl had become entered the room.

Chapter 38

Her mother's face had remained remarkably accurate in Paige's memory. It was somewhat thinner in the cheeks now and creased deeper with age, but her eyes, vivid and clear, looked at Paige now with the same love they had held in the sober times. There was *nothing* that could have erased that from her memory—not time, not even the pain that her mother's addiction had caused. Underneath it all, that look of love was the one thing she knew was real. It was the one thing that countered the weakness and the lies and the broken promises. It had been enough for Paige to keep the secret all these years.

Geri rose from the chair as Paige approached the table, but the officer motioned for her to sit. She reached her hand across the top of the table and grasped Paige's handcuffed hands. Her eyes began to water. "I'm so sorry, Annie." She fingered the metal of the cuff. "I don't expect you to forgive me, but I never meant to hurt you."

"I know," Paige replied. "I've probably always known that."

"You have no reason to believe me this time, after all the broken promises, but I will never hurt you again."

"It doesn't matter now, Mom."

"Yes, it does," she said, her face brightening momentarily. "You'll see this time. I'll take care of things."

"There's nothing for you to do now. I'll take care of it. I've been taking care of myself for a long time. The detective said that you aren't drinking anymore and you've been taking good care of yourself. You just keep doing that, okay?"

"I've thought about you every day. I knew I'd never be able to make it up to you for being a terrible mother, but it helped me to get better to think about finding you and showing you that I could be a better person. I never thought it would be like this."

"I always knew it could. I lived with that possibility every day." She saw tears forming again in her mother's eyes. "But there was no choice to make, Mom. We didn't make choices. You didn't choose to be an addict. The consequences weren't things you sat down one day and chose. You didn't knowingly choose an abuser. And I had no other choice than to run."

Tears now ran a steady stream down Geri's cheeks. She gripped Paige's hands tightly. "Did I do it? Annie, tell me. I have to know. I did it, didn't I?"

Whether or not to answer that question had already been decided. The debate had taken place in her head all the way through Illinois. Who had the best chance of winning a case, a frightened teenager or a drunk? Who would fare better in prison if they lost? Who had struggled hardest to put their life together? Who should have the shot at happiness? Ultimately, the decision had been an easy one.

Paige pushed the chair back and stood, but her eyes never left her mother's. "I'm okay," she said, backing toward the door. "And I love you."

With her pain dulled by a full dose of medication, Marissa smoothed the long, clinging skirt over her knees and waited for Moni to return. From her seat in the waiting area, she could see officers coming and going, and a handcuffed prisoner being walked across the hall. She was lost in thought when Moni reclaimed the seat next to her.

"Nothing yet," Moni informed her. "We'll just have to wait." When there was no response from Marissa, she asked, "Thinking about Paige?"

"Oh," she replied with a frown and motioned toward the hall. "I was trying to put myself in those handcuffs. I can't imagine what Paige is going through."

"Fortunately or unfortunately, she's had a training ground that has prepared her better than you or me."

"I'd do anything to spare her from this."

"Even trade places with her?"

She looked at Moni before responding. "Wouldn't that be the ultimate expression of love?" She paused in thought. "Would I be saying yes because I know that that isn't possible?"

"But Paige *can*, and she is, for her mother."

"I thought I understood sacrifice—what it means to live it, what it feels like to wonder about life without it. I doubted that someone like Paige could ever understand what that meant in my life." Marissa shook her head. "I'm the one who didn't understand, about real sacrifice, and love. I don't feel worthy of that kind of love."

"Well, thankfully, we're not the ones deciding if we're worthy of being loved. The only thing we need to do is be able to accept it."

"Worthy or not," Marissa replied, "that's exactly what I plan to do."

"Right now Paige is the one who needs to feel loved. She has to know we've got her back no matter what happens."

When the door opened near the front of the hallway, Marissa pushed herself up from the bench. An officer escorted an uncuffed Paige to the counter where he exchanged some paperwork for an envelope. He handed it to Paige and directed her toward Moni and Marissa.

Paige closed the distance quickly, hugged Moni, then wrapped Marissa in a tight embrace. "I love you," she whispered against her head. "I thought I'd never see you again."

Marissa's face shone around her smile while her eyes welled with tears. "You asked me if I was sure," she said through the tears. "I am."

"I can't ask that of you now. Not after this. There's no telling what's going to happen."

Marissa cupped Paige's face with her hands. "It's too late to be asking me anything. I'm in this with you now no matter what happens. Love's like that, you know?"

When the moment seemed appropriate, Moni asked. "What is going on? Are you free to leave?"

Page offered a questioning look. "You didn't pay bail?"

Moni shook her head.

"It seems strange that they'd even consider bail. He was one of North Branch's finest."

"What did they tell you?"

"Just to wait here. I have to talk to Detective Beaman before I leave. Nothing's making sense."

They had only a moment to wonder before Jack Beaman approached with an explanation. "Ann, you're free to go with your friends as soon as I get a statement from you. I'll wave you into that room right over there in just a few minutes."

"I don't understand," Paige replied.

"The charge has been dropped," he explained. "Your mother has confessed."

"No," Paige protested sharply. "You can't accept it." She moved in front of him as he turned to walk away. "She was too high to remember anything."

He moved around her. "I'll call you in shortly."

"Please," she pleaded, reaching out for his arm. "She passed the polygraph for God's sake."

Moni took Paige's arm as the detective walked away. "Come on, Paige."

"No, Moni. They can't do this. She's clean, she finally has a life. I can't let this happen."

"Your mother has stepped up, Paige," Moni said. "Maybe she *needs* to do this."

"Honey," Marissa stroked the side of Paige's face, "you've given her the time she needed." She turned Paige's head to face her. "You gave me the time *I* needed. It's time for you now."

"We have an attorney coming tomorrow," Moni added. "Your mother will have good representation. She was a battered woman, Paige, they'll recognize that."

Paige had no chance to respond. She was waved in to give her statement.

As Paige seated herself at the table, Jack dismissed the woman with the steno machine. "Thanks, Angie, but I'm going to have Ms. Panning write out her statement."

He placed a pad of white paper and a pen in front of Paige and settled into the chair across from her.

"Detective—"

"Begin your statement at the point on that day when you first heard or saw any interaction between your mother and your stepfather."

Paige picked up the pen and stared at the blank paper.

"Take your time," he encouraged. "Try to remember everything you can."

Paige continued to stare at the page. She *was* battered, as Moni said, for years. Threatened and frightened, stripped naked of her self-esteem. But was bellowing about cold spaghetti justification for stabbing him in the back eleven times? That's all they're going to see, all they're going to know about Geri Panning—only the physicality of a cop's murder.

"Start by *telling* me, Ann. It'll help you organize your thoughts, then you can write it down."

She focused on the pen turning between her fingers. "She called him for dinner, three times I think. He was on the back steps cleaning his gun, and drinking. I fixed dinner; Mom was too messed up to do it. He finally came in and sat down at the table, then he started yelling that his dinner was cold." She stopped and placed the pen on the tablet.

"Look at me," he directed.

She did, reluctantly.

He spoke succinctly. "Now listen very *carefully*. You are the *only* witness to what happened. Tell me what I *have* to know."

She searched his eyes, studied his face, not sure what she was looking at. What was clear was what he wanted her to say. What was not clear was *why*. He didn't pull his eyes away. There was no glint of intimidation, the lines around his eyes were soft and relaxed, the hold of his head was like she had always imagined a parent's would look like when talking with their child. He's no longer angry with me. He's not angry at all. He's in love with my mother.

"The gun was in its holster on the table beside his plate," she continued. Not a lie. "He knew I fixed the dinner. It was my fault that it was cold. His hand was on the gun as he pushed up from the table toward me." A stretch. "He was shouting and I jumped backward and knocked my chair over." The truth.

"Were you afraid for your life?"

Always. Usually. "Yes."

Jack nodded. "Go ahead."

"The rest happened so fast. He lunged forward again, bracing himself with his hands on the table, his eyes wide. Then I realized that my mother was stabbing him. He kept trying to turn around, so she kept stabbing." Maybe in her mind. "When he collapsed on the table I grabbed the knife and wrenched it from her hand. It scared me so much when he tried to get up again, that I ran from the house, threw the knife in the field, and hid in the barn. She was only trying to protect me."

"Well," he said, raising his eyebrows and tilting his head, "that's what it sounds like to me."

She could hardly believe what she was hearing. Was he accepting self-defense? What's that going to mean?

"Can you write that down for me, exactly as you've described it to me?"

"Yes, sir, I can."

"Then I'll be back in shortly to pick that up."

Thirty minutes later, Jack returned to the room, read the statement thoroughly, and placed it in the folder that he had opened hundreds of times over the years. He dropped the folder on the table face up.

Paige dropped her eyes to the large square stamp on the outside of the folder. Large black letters boldly stated CLOSED. Paige looked to Jack for confirmation.

"I don't know if you'll believe me," he said with the first smile he had offered her. "But I'm almost as glad this is over as you are."

She heard herself saying thank you over and over, and then a female officer appeared at the door with Geri. A moment later, she was holding her crying mother in her arms.

"Don't cry now," Paige whispered. "That time's gone. It's finally gone."

"I'll let you two talk," Jack said, excusing himself from the room.

Geri lifted her head from Paige's shoulder and straightened her posture. "Will you let me try, just try, to be the mother I've never been? Maybe it's too late," she said without time for Paige to reply. "I don't know if I know how. I just want to try. I might be no good at it. I—"

"One day at a time, Mom. Today you took care of me just fine." She kissed her mother's forehead. "As good as any mother could."

"There aren't enough years left for me to give you the love you missed."

"We've got today. And a brand new start." She released her mother with a smile. "Let's get out of this place," she said. "There are two special people I want you to meet." Paige took her hand and started out the door. "Then, we should probably think about taking Detective Beaman to dinner."